Who's the new hunk?

Kate Morris was curious about the cute new guy everyone was talking about. His name was Jamie Thompson. Kate thought there was something that set him apart from the rest of the kids. It was the way he looked—as if he knew a secret that no one else knew. There was no question in her mind that she and Jamie would get to know each other much, much better.

The only problem was, Jamie didn't seem to notice or care that Kate was the most popular girl in school. Was he playing hard to get? Or was that a game *she'd* be forced to play to be with the one boy she wanted?

HAMPSTEAD HIGH
HIGH
Hard To Get

Betsy
Harris

Troll Associates

Library of Congress Cataloging-in-Publication Data

Harris, Betsy.
    Hard to get / by Betsy Harris.
      p.   cm.—(Hampstead High; 1)
    Summary: Although their values clash, Kate pursues a handsome new
student who isn't immediately captivated by Kate's popularity, good
looks, and membership in the "in" crowd.
    ISBN 0-8167-1910-1
    [1. High schools—Fiction.   2. Schools—Fiction.]   I. Title.
II. Series: Harris, Betsy. Hampstead High; 1.
PZ7.H2409Har 1991
[Fic]—dc20   89-20407

A TROLL BOOK, published by Troll Associates

Printed in the United States of America.

10 9 8 7 6 5 4 3 2 1

Hard To Get

Chapter One

Kate Morris always liked the first day of school—and junior year was going to be the best ever. That's what her sister, Amy, had told her a few weeks before when she'd left for college. "That was my best year, Katie. You'll get to go to all the senior activities, but you won't have to graduate! Make it last as long as you can."

Amy had loved high school, and Kate felt exactly the same way. She was glad she had two years left. There were loads of people she knew in the senior class, so she would be able to go to their senior events but still have her own to look forward to next year. How lucky could a girl get?

She had even heard there was a great-looking new guy in town. She hadn't seen him yet, but the reports were that he was the cutest guy at Hampstead High, and possibly the cutest guy on the planet. No one fitting that description went by as Kate filled her new locker with the things she'd be needing every day: a mirror, a makeup bag, the cheerleading practice schedule she'd gotten over the summer, a bag of M&M's, a rain poncho, and a picture of her favorite actor. She was adjusting everything when her friend Beth Patterson came up.

"Leave some room for books, Kate," Beth laughed, looking at Kate's home-away-from-home locker. "You won't need that either," she added, pointing to the star-crush picture. "We've got the real thing right here at Hampstead High, and Jeannie gave me all his vital statistics."

"So I heard," Kate said. She and Beth were miles apart when it came to boys. Beth was always dreaming about some guy or other at school that Kate didn't see anything special in.

"Well, I only saw him once," Beth began, "but it was love at first sight. His name is Jamie Thompson, he's from Mayview, and he was a star player on their JV football team. His parents rented a house on Miller Avenue, but they want to buy something closer to town."

"What's his shoe size?" Kate answered. She had never been the type to get all excited over guys the way Beth did.

"There he is!" Beth whispered as she and Kate rounded the corner on the way to their first class. "Didn't I tell you he was gorgeous? I saw him first," she added plaintively.

Kate looked around without seeming to. "Which one are you talking about?"

"Let's follow him, then you'll see," Beth said, grabbing Kate's arm. Beth had a habit of tracking guys who caught her eye, and usually Kate hung back. She was more used to guys following *her*.

But this time she was curious. She knew all of the best guys in her school already; she'd dated a lot of them. If there was one tiny cloud on the horizon of her junior year, it was that none of the boys she knew was a heartbreaker. She had never really fallen for anyone yet, and she knew it wasn't going to happen with Kev Williams, or Billy Hutton, or any of the other guys she'd probably be having dates with. So this new boy made her more curious than usual.

The two girls were gaining on a tall boy who ambled along as if he were in the middle of a meadow instead of the noisy halls of Hampstead High. No, he wasn't the cutest guy on the planet, but he came close! Kate tried not to stare too hard, but she couldn't help noticing the way his hair brushed the top of his shirt collar in the nicest way. If she could only get a better look at more than his profile. Since she wasn't in the habit of staring at boys, she'd have to wait.

By then, the cute mystery guy had dropped far behind them. "He doesn't even act as if he's *got* a class in two minutes like the rest of us. We'd better get to English," Beth sighed. Kate wanted to take one last glance back, but forced herself to look straight ahead.

When they got to class, the two girls settled down at adjoining desks and reached for their books. Kate looked up at the wall clock. *Eight thirty-nine and twenty seconds*, she thought. *In ten more seconds Mrs. Griffith will come through the door and say, "Morning all." In forty seconds the bell will ring, and I'll be starting the first class of my first day in my third year at Hampstead.*

Mrs. Griffith walked through the door. "Morning all," she said brightly. A few students managed to mumble back a greeting.

Three seconds behind her, the cute mystery guy ambled in and went to the back of the room, beating the bell with seconds to spare. Kate stared after him in amazement, then whispered to Beth, "How did he do that? He was miles behind us in the hall, and at the rate he was going, he wouldn't have even made it by nine-fifteen if he was lucky."

"Track star?" Beth shrugged. "Magician?"

"I guess." Kate was dying to turn around again to get another look at the speedy, cute mystery guy. She was very impressed, but the school bell cut off the possibility of any more glances.

"All right, class," Mrs. Griffith said, "there are some preliminary announcements I have to make." She cleared her throat. "The deadline for entering the write-off…"

…*has been extended to November fifteenth.* Kate finished the sentence in her mind. They always had to extend the deadline for the essay contest in order to drum up more student interest in it.

Mrs. Griffith continued, "And the Honor Society is pleased to welcome two new members from the junior class: Mary Lou Jenkins and Jamie Thompson, transfers from Mayview." She continued to go through the announcements.

Kate scrawled a note to Beth: "Cute *and* smart." Beth scrawled back: "Don't forget speedy."

"…and the meeting of the civics club will be held on Thursday," Mrs. Griffith concluded, and plunked the sheaf of announcements down on her desk. She looked up at the class, smiled, and said, "Now, we can get started. Please turn to page twelve in your books."

Books clumped. Pages ruffled as thirty-two students searched for the right place.

Kate flipped open her book. She wished that she

had eyes in the back of her head to see what Jamie was doing. She hated that he could see her but she couldn't see him, because it made her feel as if he had an advantage over her. Her eyes roamed across the text of a poem by William Blake.

Mrs. Griffith sounded really up. "Kate Morris, would you please read the first line of 'The Lamb' for us."

Kate was used to being called on by teachers. They had been noticing her, praising her, and rewarding her since first grade. And high school hadn't been any different. She was a good student— bright and curious. But "The Lamb" taxed her patience a bit. She liked poetry, but not this kind— about a woolly lamb "making all the vales rejoice." *Give me a break,* she thought. Nevertheless, she read the first stanza in her clear voice.

Mrs. Griffith beamed at her. Kate knew she was one of the teacher's favorites, because they'd gotten to know each other when Kate was elected secretary of the Spanish club. "Thank you, Kate. Very nice," she said. She scanned the room for a few seconds. "Jamie Thompson, would you please read the next stanza."

Kate smiled at herself. Now she'd get to hear the actual speaking voice of the cute guy. *Too bad he's not speaking to me.*

Jamie had a really nice voice. Kind of soft and low and strong. Even the stuff about "I a child, and thou a lamb" didn't sound dumb the way Jamie read it.

"Thank you, Jamie," Mrs. Griffith said and proceeded to lead the class into a long discussion about Blake and his life and poetry. It didn't feel like an exciting start of things to Kate—she waited for the bell, which finally rang, releasing the class from the woolly lamb stuff.

"C'mon, what are you waiting for?" Beth asked.

Kate answered with exaggerated composure, "I'm just making sure I have all my books and notes." She was deliberately rearranging them on top of one another.

"Very cute," Beth said with a knowing smile. "Making sure you 'happen' to run into our friend."

Kate grinned. "Well, he doesn't move super-fast, so I thought I'd kill some time with this." She reshuffled her papers once more.

"Don't look now, but guess who's waiting in the hall?" Beth said.

Kate looked up and gathered everything in her arms. She saw Jamie outside the classroom door. "How does he do that?" she laughed. "It's as if he can appear and disappear whenever he wants. I swear he was in the back of the room a few seconds ago."

The two girls went out into the chaos of the hall. Kate thought there was something about Jamie that set him apart from the rest of the kids—made him seem different. It wasn't just his height; he was close to six feet tall, she thought. No, it was the way he looked—as if he knew a secret that no one else knew. *Yes*, she said to herself, *this is someone I'm really going to enjoy being with.* There was no question in her mind that she and Jamie would get to know each other much, much better.

"Hi," he greeted the two girls. "Tell me something. Are all the classes going to be like this—

reading aloud?" He had directed his question to Kate.

She smiled back at his lazy grin. He seemed so relaxed as he leaned against one of the lockers—as if he had nothing to do for the rest of the day but rehash Mrs. Griffith's class. Kate smoothed some stray strands of her wavy hair off her face and said, "It's the way she always starts things, I heard. My sister had her and said she's really great once she gets going."

"What's your next class?" he asked Kate. He acted as if they had known each other for a long time.

"I know what my next class is," Beth said breathlessly. "And I'm going to be late for it unless I split right now. See you guys." She waved to Kate as she disappeared down the hall.

"I've got Basic IIA," Kate said.

Jamie seemed impressed. "That's an advanced computer class, isn't it?"

"Yes. And if I don't head for it now," she said, "I'll be late—it's in the other building."

"Great. You can show me the way." Jamie smiled down at her.

Kate didn't get it for a few seconds. "Are you in that class too?" *He must be,* she thought. *The only other classes in that building are sophomore biology and freshman chemistry.*

"Yeah. Are you surprised?" They were now walking side by side down the hall as if they had always known each other.

"Not really," she answered. "After all, you are a member in good standing of the Honor Society."

She said it in a kind of teasing voice.

"I don't know how good my standing is, but you're right," he said.

Kate noticed that she had fallen in step with him and was strolling along at the same laid-back pace. *How does he get* anywhere *on time?* She figured she'd ask. "Do you mind if I ask you a couple of things?"

Before he could answer, two girls and a guy came up to Kate. "Kate, how's it going?" the girls greeted her. "Hey, Kate, how're you doing?" the boy asked, as if he hadn't seen her for a long time. Billy Hutton always acted this way with Kate.

Kate smiled back warmly. "I'm great, you guys, how's everything?" She turned to Jamie, planning to introduce him to her friends. She laughed. "You know, of course, that you and I don't officially know each other."

"Sure we do," he answered with a grin. "We just went through a semi-draggy English class together, and we've been walking to Basic IIA. What more do you want?" he teased.

"Your name might be nice for starters," she answered. Beth had already mentioned his name, but Kate didn't want *him* to know that.

He grinned his cute grin. "I'm Jamie Thompson."

"Bye, Katie," the girls said as they turned to go. "See you later—we'll save a place for you at lunch." Billy seemed reluctant to leave. "Bye, Kate. See you."

Before Kate and Jamie could continue their conversation, another guy and girl stopped Kate. "Katie, we've got to get together to go over the homecoming stuff. It's already a huge mess," the girl said.

"It always is," Kate acknowledged. "We've only been back here for about an hour. Give me a little more time." She started to introduce Jamie.

"Okay, but we definitely have to talk soon," the girl said as they hurried away.

"Now do you mind if I ask *you* a couple of things?" Jamie said.

"I don't know." Kate smiled. "I didn't get a chance to ask you my questions yet." She'd die before she asked him stuff she *really* wanted to know—like, Do you have a girlfriend? Do you think I'm pretty? Do you like me a little?—so she just answered, "I guess you can. Go ahead."

"How many things are you involved in? Forty-three?" he teased.

Did he think she was weird? Oh no, they'd only known each other—if you could call it that—for a few minutes and she was worrying about proving herself to him. But she figured he was only teasing, so she shrugged and answered, "Not quite, but a lot."

"Like what?"

"Like cheerleading and the Spanish club and the homecoming committee and—"

"Stop. I've heard enough already." He threw his hands up in mock horror.

"It's fun," she protested. *It always has been*, she thought to herself with the faintest glimmering of doubt in the back of her mind.

"I guess so," he said, and looked at her a little more closely than he had before.

9

Kate didn't understand what his look meant. Was he registering her on his weird meter? Or was he more interested in her than he seemed? She couldn't tell. Oh well, she really liked what she knew about him so far—which wasn't much. She decided to ask him the secret of his getting from one place to another. "It's my turn to ask you something now."

"I hope it's harder than the last one about my name."

"I was just being super-polite," she teased back. "No. What I want to know is, how do you manage to get around from class to class?"

"What do you mean?"

"You have noticed, of course, that everyone else seems to hurtle along the halls at one hundred and twelve miles an hour." She paused to see his reaction. He still had the same quiet smile on his face, so she continued. "And you proceed at about four miles an hour."

"Oh that," he laughed. "It's my Zzekes and Zzopes routine."

"What?" At first she didn't pick up on the names of the cartoon characters Jamie was talking about.

"You know how Zzopes is always running around like a crazy person all the time?"

"Yeah," Kate answered. "I still don't get it."

"Zzekes is much more laid back—at least he tries to be," Jamie continued. "Anyway, he's always arriving before Zzopes does, because Zzopes has wasted so much time being in a hurry." He grinned at her with a look of satisfaction.

Kate wasn't entirely convinced. "You mean you

10

get where you're going faster by going slower?" She frowned at him. "Sounds more like zen than Zzekes and Zzopes to me."

"Actually, I made the whole theory up." He laughed. "It has to do with the laws of physics. You see—"

Kate grimaced at him. "*Please*—don't tell me any more. I've heard more than I need to." What kind of guy was he anyway?

"You did ask me," he countered.

"Guilty as charged," she admitted, and looked at one of the clocks lining the halls. "I don't think your Zzekes and Zzopes routine is working right now." She grabbed his arm. "We've got three minutes to get all the way over to The Tomb."

"The what?"

"The Tomb. It's a nickname for the old building," she answered.

"I can't think of anyone I'd rather be buried with." Jamie laughed.

Chapter Two

"How come you're taking Basic IIA?" Kate asked, trying to keep pace with Jamie. He had obviously listened to her advice about speeding up on the way to The Tomb. She felt a tiny twinge of pride that something as small as that had made an impression on him. She stopped herself. *Why should I care whether he pays attention to what I say or not?* But Kate was already beginning to get the answer. Anyone who looked the way he did, and was also a football star, and smart too...she knew she'd be weird *not* to care.

"I started working out this program," Jamie began to answer almost to himself—then he smiled at Kate. "It was great: a computer music program that I didn't have a chance to finish over the summer..."

Kate wanted to ask him what he had done during the past months that had interfered with his computer work, but she didn't want to seem too curious or nosy. Anyway, boys were always coming up to her at the beginning of the school year telling her what they'd done over the summer. Sometimes it seemed that a few of them—like Jack Durham and Billy Hutton—made their vacations sound as if they'd been asked to join some famous spy for a few weeks of fun. They liked to show off for laughs. She had a feeling that Jamie wouldn't go that far, but she was pretty sure he'd be anxious to tell her more about himself. At least she *hoped* so.

"Hey, Kate," an athletic-looking blond guy called to her with a smile. "Good to see you." It was Tim McMullen, and he looked as if he wanted to talk to Kate; but he was coming from one direction as Kate and Jamie were speed-walking in the other.

Kate beamed back. She was glad that Jamie could see she was pretty popular with boys. He was noticing, of course, wasn't he? She flicked a tiny glance toward him, but his face revealed nothing more than the same friendly expression it had when she first saw him. "Hey, Tim," she answered back over her shoulder, "how was it?" She knew he'd gone on one of those wilderness survival trips over the summer.

"Unbelievable. I'll tell you about it at lunch," he said eagerly. "I'll save you a seat."

"Another name for your dance card," Jamie grinned.

"Huh? I don't get it," Kate said. "What's my dance card?" Was this something he was making up to tease her?

"You know," he prodded. "It was a card that girls carried on their wrists—or wherever..." He looked at her. "Come on. You know what it is—you're putting me on."

Kate felt the faintest blush cross her cheeks. Why didn't she know what the dumb dance card was anyway? Still, she answered evenly, "I'm not

14

kidding. Dance cards aren't the latest craze at Hampstead." She managed to sound poised in spite of the fact that she now felt super-stupid about the whole thing.

"Well, a man would ask a woman for a dance and she'd write his name on her card." He was explaining it as if it were something that every kid knew about. "So a really popular girl would have a full dance card."

"Nice," Kate said. She didn't want to sound too excited or bored by the dance card stuff.

"From what I've seen, you'd need a dance card that was three feet long." Jamie smiled but he didn't sound awed or impressed.

He's talking about my popularity the same way he'd talk about the weather, thought Kate. She tried to think of other guys at Hampstead who would act the way Jamie did. Especially a new kid at school. But Jamie didn't really act "new." He acted as if he'd known Kate all through high school—had walked down these halls with her hundreds of times. She wondered about his three-foot-long dance card remark and said a little flirtatiously, "I don't know where I'd keep something like that— especially at a dance."

He looked at her with an almost imperceptible smile. "A smart girl like you would figure something out," he answered.

Why did he look at her like that? Why did she care? She'd just met him, after all. "I hope so" was all she decided to answer.

The two of them were getting closer to Mr. Samuel's computer class. Even though it was one of Kate's favorite classes, she suddenly wished that she and Jamie hadn't walked so quickly, gotten to their destination so fast. There was more she wanted to say—more she needed to hear. She wanted to hear about Jamie's summer, and even how he knew about the dance cards that had made her feel that she definitely didn't have the upper hand with him. But she'd have to wait. Meanwhile, she turned to Jamie as they got to the door and explained, "The seating in this class is alphabetical, so I guess I'll see you later." She hoped that he'd want to sit next to her, but all he said was "Thanks."

Computer class was great—a series of problems and challenges that Kate loved working on. She even forgot about Jamie as she peered at the screen in front of her and darted the cursor back and forth rapidly. It was only when the bell rang and she had to leave that she realized Jamie had been in the same room all along. She figured they'd walk back from The Tomb together, but Kate saw Jamie amble out of the classroom while she greeted Janie Sherry, Greg Kirby, and a few more kids she hadn't seen over the summer.

"How was your summer?" Janie asked.

Kate gathered up her books and looked at the empty doorway through which Jamie had disappeared. "Everything was great." She felt as if catching up with Jamie was something she *had* to do. "I'll talk to you guys later. See you." She hurried off.

The halls of The Tomb were narrower—and more crowded—than those in the new building. Kate couldn't pick Jamie out of the swarms of kids walking, shoving, running along. She picked up her pace. *Why had he walked off like that?*

16

Doesn't he like me? Did I mess up somehow because I didn't know about the dumb dance card? Where is he? There he is! He was alone. She felt a small sigh of relief. The rugby shirt that stretched loosely across his shoulders seemed oddly reassuring to her. As long as she could see him, he seemed to belong to her somehow. Her eyes lingered on the hair that brushed his collar. She smiled and caught up until she was a few paces behind him, then slowed down a bit so it would look as if she were as casual and unhurried as he. Kate even considered walking by him, pretending she hadn't noticed him. *Don't be dumb,* she told herself and fell in step beside Jamie.

"Isn't Samuel's class great?" she asked.

"Yeah, pretty good," he agreed.

"What have you got next period?"

He paused for a second. "Let me see." His face brightened. "Oh yeah. Mr. Guest's class, 'Images Through Words.'"

Kate almost stopped short. Jamie probably didn't know that everyone's nickname for the class was "Terror Through Words," and that Mr. Guest had a reputation unrivaled by Frankenstein. He was considered one of the toughest—and the best—teachers at Hampstead. If you wanted to keep your average up, you stayed out of his classes.

"He's pretty tough," Kate offered.

Jamie didn't seem surprised. "Yeah. The transfer counselor told me that too—almost like a warning."

Kate expanded. "Oh, you have no idea. Getting an A from Guest is like getting blood from a stone." She corrected herself. "Come to think of it, getting the blood from a stone would be a snap compared to getting an A."

Jamie looked puzzled and shrugged his shoulders. "I don't get it. Why would kids stay away from a class just because the teacher's tough? Especially a guy like Guest, who everyone says is great?"

Was this guy for real? "But what about keeping up your average? Staying in the Honor Society?"

"I just want to get the best that's offered." Jamie didn't seem to understand Kate's point at all. "I'll take a B—or even a C—if it means having a guy like Guest." He looked down at her. "Haven't you been in his classes?"

Kate felt kind of small. "I was in 'Terror'—I mean 'Images'—for a few weeks, but I asked to transfer out."

"Why?"

She answered softly, "Because I wasn't sure I could pull an A in it—and the grade was really important to me." Why did she feel as if she were on the witness stand? Was it so wrong to want a good grade? "I was only a sophomore."

"Whatever," Jamie said evenly. He continued, "What have you got next?"

"Comp IV." Ordinarily, Kate would have felt really proud of herself. It was an advanced English class, but the teacher was a pretty good grader. "I like Miss Anderson." She glanced up at Jamie. "I've got to hustle—I don't have a Zzekes and Zzopes routine like yours. I'll see you at lunch."

"Should I make a reservation to be at your table?" he teased. "Or were all the seats booked last May?"

Kate couldn't tell from his tone whether he was serious about wanting to get together or whether he was teasing her. She decided to avoid an answer and waved to Jamie as she took the stairs two at a time.

The Hampstead cafeteria sounded like a cross between a super-packed Burger King and an amped-up disco. Radios weren't supposed to be played loud, but the kids who decided to forgo earphones in favor of blasters made sure everyone knew they were around. The sound of 318 kids talking and laughing clashed with music, trays, cutlery, and dishes. Everyone hated the place—and loved it—because lunch was one of the main events of the day. It was the time to catch up on everything: boyfriends, teachers, girlfriends, break-ups, and make-ups.

"Here, Kate, I've got a place for you," Janie Sherry called.

Kate waved, smiled back, and said with a mock grimace, "Sorry, I've got to go over some stuff about homecoming." She nodded her head in a direction two tables away from Janie and made her way to a table already filling up with some of the best-looking kids at Hampstead.

"Here she is," a handsome guy said as he pulled out a chair he'd been saving for Kate.

"Thanks, Cal." She settled into the chair and gave him a warm smile. "How's everything?" she asked him, knowing that he wouldn't really talk about himself. Cal Brooks was kind of shy in spite of his looks.

"Pretty much the same," he answered in a soft voice. "How was your summer? I called you a couple of weeks ago, but your mother said you were visiting your grandparents."

Kate took a delicate bite from the chicken salad in front of her. "Yes, I just got back a few days before school." She didn't want to apologize for not returning the call, because Cal was a nice guy—but not someone Kate felt like encouraging. She found herself wondering where Jamie was right now. She looked around at the tables near her, expecting to see him somewhere in the area. After all, the Hampstead cafeteria was divided and sub-divided by invisible barriers and lines: seniors here, juniors there, jocks here, dips there, cheerleaders next to the jocks, computer whizzes next to the dips, and on and on until everyone was slotted in a place. No one strayed much from his or her "territory." Kate sometimes felt that the system was too rigid, too confining, but she shrugged off her doubts. After all, wasn't it the way things had always been? And she didn't *really* want to sit with David Knapp and his band of computer nerds. Still, she wondered why she wasn't able to spot Jamie—even he would probably conform to the unwritten cafeteria rule of "a place for everyone, and everyone in his place."

"Earth calling Kate," Bonnie Sims laughed.

Kate didn't realize she'd been tuned out of the conversation. "Sorry, what?"

"I was asking you about the theme for homecoming," Bonnie said. "Cal thinks a movie theme is too expensive to do."

"To do right," he corrected. "Aren't you getting tired of that tinfoil stuff that looks like the Christmas candy display at Woolworth's?"

"Well, do you have any better suggestions?"

20

Bonnie sniffed, adding with a flirtatious smile, "Mr. Super Special Effect/Movie Director rolled into one handsome package."

Kate tuned them out and scanned the cafeteria. He had made the joke about reserving a seat at her table. Suddenly she saw him—sitting with some guys from the band. What was he doing over there? With *them*? Didn't he know that they were really out of it? Couldn't he tell? She realized with a little sigh that he had been joking about sitting with her, and rejoined the conversation about the homecoming dance.

"You guys know that space stuff really is pretty steep to pull off," she said. "Why don't we go back to that idea of the music video theme I told you about last spring? You know, with the giant rock superstar posters—and the special lights that Mr. Hardesty offered to set up for us."

"That sounds great," Bonnie said happily.

"Yeah. Did you really get Hardesty to fork over the lights?" Some of Cal's shyness faded when he was involved in projects. "Did you promise to take up carpentry and wiring as hobbies?"

Kate grimaced, and said with mock solemnity, "Sure. And he told me he'd give the entire junior class a trip to Europe just because *I'm* such a nice, polite girl—not like some of those other kids who've gone to his store." She imitated the hardware store owner's gruff voice. "Seriously, he's okay. All I did was ask him, and he was really nice about it. Said yes—offered to have one of the guys who worked in the store set things up." She shrugged. "It was a piece of cake." To Kate it was. The way it had always been: just ask—and you receive. Most of the time that's the way it worked for her.

"Maybe we can get Hardesty to pay for refreshments for homecoming," Cal offered.

"Get real, Cal." Kate smiled. She had been picking at her lunch; between planning the dance and secretly eyeing Jamie, she had scarcely eaten anything. Then as she was raising a forkful of the chicken salad to her mouth, she saw him get up from the table and start toward the tray dropoff. She put her fork down and got up as quickly and casually as she could. She didn't want anyone to know that she was even the least bit interested in Jamie, even if he was super-cute. He was a new kid at school. *New*, she reminded herself. *I only met him this morning and have had a total of about two and one-half conversations with him. Why am I acting like this about him?* She tuned out her own thoughts before she got an answer, picked up her tray, and said, "Sorry, you guys, I've got to go over some of the exercises for Mademoiselle Duchamp's class. See ya."

"Don't go yet, Kate," Bonnie moaned. "We have to finish some more homecoming stuff."

Jamie had stopped and was talking to Brian Winter, who was holding up a small book and laughing with Jamie about it before he handed it to him.

"I'll take your tray up for you, Kate," Cal offered.

She glanced back at Cal. "Thanks. I need the exercise," she teased, and walked toward the dropoff. When she arrived there just alongside Jamie, she pretended not to see him.

"Hi. Guess you didn't reserve me a place, did you?" he asked with a slow, lazy smile.

22

Kate felt like saying the same thing back, but she couldn't bring herself to utter a lie as big as that. Who would ever want to reserve a seat with the band? Some of the guys—especially Brian Winter—were kind of cute, but...the band?! Too different... too musical...or artsy...or something. Definitely not Kate's crowd, but she was curious about how Jamie had hooked up with them instead of, say, the football team. Surely, he had more in common with them. "How do you know Brian Winter?" she asked.

"A friend of mine from Mayview is a good friend of his," Jamie answered. "They were in a national band competition together."

"That's nice," Kate answered evenly. *Maybe the Mayview High School Band isn't considered as dippy as ours,* she thought. She and Jamie fell in step together as they left the cafeteria. She loved walking next to him, but as she gave him a quick glance, she couldn't tell how he felt about her at all.

Chapter Three

It was October twentieth and the leaves were turning. School had been going on for six weeks. Kate saw Jamie every day. She laughed with him in the classes they shared and teased him when she saw him in the halls. *He's fun, he's cute, he's smart*, she said to herself as she stuffed her gym suit onto the top shelf of her locker. *But I don't understand him.* She'd never met any boy like him—most guys who'd been friendly to her asked her out sooner or later.

"Hey, Kate," Beth greeted her. "Do you believe the ton of homework Jacobs piled on us?" She kicked an extra pair of aqua plastic flats into the back of her locker. "Never mind answering, 'cause I know that you got it done like that." She snapped her fingers. "On to question number two: Have you turned down any invitations for homecoming?"

Kate laughed. "What do you think I am—a date machine?"

"I don't know what that is exactly," Beth answered, "but if it means someone who *sometimes* has more dates than she needs, then *yes!*" She straightened the braided cotton band that wound through her hair and twisted some of the curls into different directions. "You know, I'm not sure that getting this body wave was the smartest thing in the world. Sometimes I think my hair looks more like that picture of Louis the Fourteenth in our history books than a cover girl."

Kate shook her head. She had never known Beth to stay on the same subject for more than forty seconds at a time—unless the subject happened to be one of Beth's new crushes. "Your hair does *not* look like Louis the Fourteenth's." She grabbed her friend's arm. "C'mon, let's go."

Beth snuck a last look at her hair in the mirror hanging on her locker door and stuck her tongue out at herself. She slammed the door shut. "You didn't update me on the homecoming situation. Tell all."

"There's no 'all' to tell. The only guy I turned down was Scott Welles."

"You didn't!" Beth moaned. "But he's so cute."

"*He* thinks so," Kate emphasized. She noticed the slightly hurt look on Beth's face. "I know you had a big crush on him last spring, Beth." She paused a bit. "He really is okay. It's just that he sometimes acts so conceited about his looks." She wished she could add that he wasn't at all like Jamie, who acted as if he *never* looked in the mirror, and if he did—well, his was just another face. But Kate would never let on to anyone— not even Beth—how she felt about Jamie. Beth would only come up with a hundred crazy schemes for getting and keeping Jamie's attention and undying affection and devotion.

Beth was still pouting a little about Scott Welles.

"You could have given him a little chance, don't you think?"

"I don't call the homecoming dance a 'little' chance," Kate sighed. "It's a pretty big event." Jamie's face flashed through her mind. She'd give anything to go with him, but he hadn't asked her out—yet.

"It's too bad that Jamie Thompson turned out to be so weird," Beth said. She gave Kate a genuinely puzzled look. "You'd think a guy like that wouldn't hang around with the creeps he does."

"They're not creeps," Kate said defensively.

Beth stopped walking. "Since when were the 'lits' and the band considered so great?"

She didn't have an answer for Beth. She didn't really disagree with her, but she hated to hear anything connected with Jamie called creepy. "They're just not like us," she said lamely.

Beth resumed walking. "That's exactly what I mean. They aren't like us at all, and it seemed as if Jamie really was like us." She shook her head. "A guy who looks like that and was a JV football star at Mayview—the county champions. What kind of guy is he anyway?" She didn't wait for any answer. "Tim McMullen told me he didn't even try out for football, just soccer."

"I know," Kate said softly. She couldn't figure it out either. "Maybe he got tired of it."

Beth looked at her as if she were from outer space. "*Tired* of being a football star?" she said incredulously. "Just the way Tim gets tired of being cheered at every game, being mobbed by all the girls, and being one of the most popular guys around. All the jocks *hate* that stuff. Right?"

"Oh, I don't know," Kate said. "Besides, I don't really care if Jamie Thompson is a football star or not. I mean, he's just another guy," she lied. She cared *too* much. In the past six weeks that she'd known him, he had proved to be anything but just another guy. The only things she could predict about him had to do with the classes they shared. Everything else—his friends, his free time, even his clothes—were full of surprises. She knew she'd see him in another two minutes before English. She pictured him in jeans with his Mozart T-shirt and black hightop sneakers—not the hot kind, just dippy old Sears hightops.

Beth nudged her. "Speaking of our friend,"—she nodded toward Jamie, who was going at his own pace, just the way he had the first day the two girls had seen him.

Today he was dressed like someone from *The Preppy Handbook.* He had on a pretty blue polo shirt, jeans, and a soft green shetland tied carelessly around his shoulders. Kate checked his sneakers. It was a day for Nikes. Her eyes traveled back up from his feet, and she admired him all over again as if she were seeing him for the first time.

Beth didn't even seem to care much about Jamie. She glanced casually at him, said "Hi," then turned to Kate and said, "I'll see you after class."

Kate was glad Beth had to leave. She was sure that someday soon Jamie was going to ask her out. *Maybe he's shy*, she thought. She vowed right then to write her older sister, Amy, and ask her for advice about the whole Jamie thing. She'd know what to do.

Jamie grinned at Kate with the smile that she always felt must mean something more. "How far did you get on the assigned reading?"

"Not as far as you, I bet," she answered with a twinkle. She loved his eyes. They were deep blue with flecks of smoky gray in them. *He's cuter than anyone,* she decided, *because he's not too pretty. It's the gray flecks and the crooked grin that do it,* she thought.

"I asked you first," he prodded with a smile. "I like to keep up with the competition."

Well, at least he thinks I'm smart. His remark relaxed her. Lately, whenever she saw Jamie, Kate felt a mixture of happiness, relief, and nervousness. She wasn't used to feeling nervous around boys. It was usually *she* who made *them* nervous. "I got up to page ninety-seven."

"I knew it!" Jamie answered, pretending he was angry. "Last night I tied myself to my chair. No, that's not true," he corrected. "I had the dog tie me to the chair. And you've never seen anything more pitiful than my dog when he tries to be useful with the clothesline."

"I know what you mean," Kate said. "My cat, Muffin, is hopeless when it comes to cleaning up my room."

"There I was—lashed to the chair, eyes riveted on *Voyages in English: Supplementary Reading, Volume Three.*" He paused, faking breathlessness as if he were describing a horse race. "Page eighty-nine, ninety, ninety-one, ninety-two. Top of ninety-three, bottom of ninety-three, top of ninety-four, middle of ninety-four." His voice slowed and softened. "I couldn't do it. I couldn't make it past the middle of ninety-four. I beat my fists on the book and told Ollie to untie me."

"Who's Ollie?"

"The dog who's not good with the clothesline."

"Of course, I should have known." Kate half believed that Jamie had a weird dog who could do rope tricks.

"Then I said to Ollie, 'You know, pal, tomorrow when I ask Kate Morris how far she got in this stuff, I *know* she'll be ahead of me.'"

"And what did Ollie say?" Kate loved these moments with Jamie. He could be so much fun.

"He just barked sympathetically and told me it was no big deal for the nicest girl in the class to be the smartest."

Kate's heart caught in her throat. Jamie had said things like that before, but it was different from the way she'd heard other boys say it. His compliments almost weren't compliments—just statements of fact. He didn't use them to flirt—at least not as far as Kate could tell. He was just being nice. "Ollie sounds very smart. Do you think he'd help me do my homework sometime?"

"Sure, I'll have him give you a call," Jamie grinned. "But it's hard for him to get his paws on the right buttons. He's a sheepdog."

"I love sheepdogs, they're the same..."

The bell for class cut off the rest of Kate's comments about Ollie, but not her thoughts about Jamie. *Will you listen to yourself,* she cautioned. *Hoping a dog will help a guy call!* You *need help.* She almost wrote to Amy during class, but she was too busy answering Mrs. Griffith's questions.

Cheerleading practice ended late, and Kate was rushing back to her locker to change. She had promised her little sister, Connie, that she'd take her shopping for some jeans, and she didn't want to keep her waiting long. Kate decided to take a short-cut that went past the warren of rooms used for extracurricular activities like the school clubs, paper, and yearbook.

She almost screeched to a halt when she saw Jamie poring over a chessboard opposite Mandy Harris in one of the rooms. Chess?! Mandy Harris?! The only girl—the only student—at Hampstead who knew everything about physics, almost more than her teacher. She was also the only student who knew practically *nothing* about clothes. Kate *had* to go in.

"Hi," she said casually.

The two hadn't seen her come in and looked up, startled. Mandy retained the same grim-serious expression on her face that she'd had when she was playing chess. Jamie grinned and seemed genuinely glad to see Kate. "Hi. You know Mandy, don't you?"

"Sure," Kate said. The two girls looked at each other as if they were creatures from different solar systems. Mandy managed to give Kate a tight smile.

"How come you're here so late?" Jamie asked. He wasn't kidding.

"I had cheerleading practice. We have a big game coming up on Saturday."

Jamie's expression crossed between chagrin

and laughter as he noticed Kate's cheerleading outfit. "I'm not very observant right now, am I?"

Mandy continued to stare at Kate. As a matter of fact, both she and Jamie looked expectantly at her, as if they were wondering why she'd interrupted their game. All of a sudden, Kate felt dumb and out of place standing there in her red-and-white striped outfit. Dozens of girls would have given anything to be able to wear the uniform, but right now Kate wished she were wearing something else.

Jamie gave her a warm smile. "You don't mind if Mandy and I get back to this? She's about to demolish me."

Kate twisted one of the white cords that draped across the front of her outfit. "Of course not, you guys—I just wanted to say hi," she said a little too brightly. "And also to tell you about the Weird Noise tickets." Surely *those* would interest Jamie. She had won them that morning by calling her favorite radio station.

Mandy had already turned back to the chessboard and hunched her shoulders over it.

"Are you going to the concert?" Jamie asked a little vaguely.

Kate figured it would be good to leave him in suspense. "Don't know yet. Talk to you about it later." She flashed him her brightest smile, and left.

As she walked down the hall toward her locker, she looked down at her prized cheerleader's outfit, and for a few seconds it looked like a Bozo the Clown suit. The same thoughts and questions kept whirring through her mind. Who ever heard of a football star playing chess? Who ever saw a guy who looked like Jamie hanging out with someone who looked and acted like Mandy Harris? Didn't he have a clue about what counted in school? Didn't he care what the other kids thought?

"Where did you go?" Bonnie called down the hall as Kate rounded the corner to her locker.

"I took the shortcut," Kate answered. She didn't feel like talking to anyone right now.

"I think the 'cut' wasn't so 'short.'"

"I ran into Jamie Thompson and Mandy Harris," Kate said blankly. "They were playing chess."

"Chess!" Bonnie laughed harshly. "I thought Mandy spent all her time studying to be an astronaut." She was carefully hanging her cheerleader's uniform in her locker. "Of course, chess is probably the only chance she'd get to be within two feet of someone as cute as Jamie, even if he is a little weird. Why was he playing chess?"

"I don't know," Kate answered. She still couldn't figure it out. She'd changed out of her uniform and checked her makeup in the locker mirror. *I wonder whether he thinks I'm pretty.* Neither she nor the mirror had an answer. "I've gotta hustle," she said to Bonnie. "I'm taking my sister shopping."

"Lucky her to have you for a big sister," Bonnie smiled. "See you tomorrow."

"It's for you, Kate," her mother called upstairs. "A boy," she added in a loud whisper.

Kate had ignored the ringing phone in her room because she was sitting down to write a letter to Amy and wanted to collect all the stray thoughts she had about the Jamie situation. *It could be any-one,* she figured as she picked up the phone and said in an offhand voice, "Hello."

"Hi. It's Jamie Thompson," he said as if he called every night.

Kate sat bolt upright on her bed. This was the first time he'd called. The Weird Noise tickets must have done it! She managed to sound calm. "How are you? Has Ollie done your homework for you?"

"Yeah. He's really cracking the books tonight. You should hear him recite from *Julius Caesar.*"

"I hope I didn't interrupt your chess game too much," she asked. She thought it was good to remind him of the time and place he'd heard about the Weird Noise tickets. It would give him an easy lead-in.

"No, it was okay," he answered. "Mandy completely demolished me anyway."

What am I supposed to say to that? Good for her? Bad for her? More like, who cares about her? Kate thought. She'd never known anyone who played chess—not even her father played chess. Might as well tell him the truth. "I've never known anyone who was really interested in chess."

"You haven't?" He sounded surprised. "It's great. I'll teach you sometime. It's like a combination of…" Suddenly a dog was barking loudly near the phone. "Hold on a sec, okay?"

He didn't call me to discuss chess, I hope. Before Kate finished her thought, Jamie was back on the line.

"Sorry. Ollie wanted to be let out," the familiar voice said. "He can only do so much writing at one time."

Kate wondered what Jamie's bedroom looked like. She wondered what he was wearing. Most of all, she wondered when he was going to ask her out. But instead of betraying herself, all she said was "Smart dog."

"Yeah. He's still a puppy, but he's pretty big. I think he's going to look like a small horse by the time he's grown."

Kate went along with the conversation. "When did you get him?"

"My dad got him for my little sister a couple of months ago. But she got tired of him after he outgrew the fuzzy-ball stage."

And so on. From Ollie to school, to a local demonstration to save the original City Hall, and back to chess. Jamie never mentioned the Weird Noise concert. Or any concert. Or any date.

"I shouldn't keep you on any longer," he finally said. "Not if you're going to keep ahead of me in English. I'll see you tomorrow, okay? Bye."

"Bye." Kate hung up the phone and stared at it. What kind of boy called up just to talk? Not to ask about homework. Not to find out about a class meeting. Not to ask her out. *Just to talk!* Kate had plenty to ask Amy.

Chapter Four

Kate burrowed under the pink and raspberry quilted comforter on her bed and fluffed the pillows up on the headboard. She began the letter to Amy with the pet nickname the family had for her.

Dear Kit:

Are you Queen of Everything yet? Is sophomore year as good as freshman? Are you still skinny? How's Cece? Say hi to her, and tell her I hope I have a roommate like her when I go to college.

No more questions for now—at least not ones about you. Mostly because I know everything is fabulous with you. I miss you an awful lot and I wish you were here to help me out. I'm not desperate or anything grim like that, just hopelessly going crazy over a guy. And it isn't that he doesn't like me—it's just (a huge "just") that he hasn't asked me out. But that's not the big thing—which is that he's really different...in a neat way, but I can't figure him out and you absolutely have got to tell me what to do. I'll start from the beginning, but I'll try and stick to the main points so this letter doesn't end up being twenty pages long.

His name is Jamie Thompson and he's dreamy-looking and smart and funny. So what's the problem, I can hear you asking. He's a transfer student from Mayview (where he was a JV football star). So you'd think he'd hang out with the jocks—right? Wrong. He didn't even go out for football. The only sport he seems interested in is soccer—and you know those guys aren't considered real jocks by anybody, not even themselves. That's not all. You should see some of the people he hangs around with—the band! Yecch. Gulp. Double yecch. I'm making it sound like Jamie's King of the Wimps—but he's not. He's really neat. He could hang around with all of us (especially me) *all* the time, but he doesn't seem interested. Can you understand that at all? He could be one of the most popular kids in school, but he doesn't seem to care. I don't understand it!

We share a few classes and he's really friendly to me, but not friendly enough—or interested enough—or whatever—to ask me out. I don't understand the rules he plays by. Any other guy who was friendly would have asked me out at least twice already. Speaking of classes, before I forget—guess what he's taking? You won't believe it—Guest's "Terror Through Words." He was surprised that I wasn't in it, so I tried to explain about grades and how Guest is allergic to A's, but it didn't seem to click with Jamie. He cares more about the class than the grade. Do you believe it?

I wish I didn't care about him at all—maybe it's the fact that he is so different from Kev and

Cal and Tim. I'm really confused, so please tell me to do one of the following (I know how busy you are, so you can just check off the answer and send it back to me):

☐ Forget him—he's too out to be in.
☐ Forget him—have fun with the guys who do ask you out.
☐ Give him one more chance, then forget him.

Some last-minute thoughts: I told him about some Weird Noise tickets I had (I won them in the KMAQ radio phone-in contest). I thought absolutely, for sure, it was the perfect chance for him to ask me. You know what he did—called me up just to talk! Who ever heard of a guy doing that? Is it possible he doesn't like Weird Noise? Unbelievable!

Sorry this letter has gone on so long, Kit. You're the only one who can help. I haven't let on to anyone (not even Beth) how I feel about Jamie. I'm not *upset*—just running around in circles.

Take care, have fun. Write when you get a chance (which means twenty-six seconds after you read this letter). Miss you.

Hugs and kisses,
Kate

PS. He plays chess!
PPS. He plays chess with Mandy Harris!! (Remember her, the science genius, first woman on the moon?)

Kate reread the letter to Amy. She thought that seeing her own words on paper might give her some clues to "the secret Jamie" or even some explanation for her own feelings. What had started out as definite interest in the "new boy in school" had blossomed into a full-blown crush—something that Kate had never really experienced. Sure, there had been boys to like before—even boys to fall in love with...for about two dates. Then it was over. Because they were too young or silly or just like everyone else. It was the last part—the sameness—that nagged at Kate. Her crowd was always going to the same parties with the same people—telling the same jokes—year in and year out. They were the most popular kids at Hampstead, so they should be the most interesting. Right? *Maybe not*, Kate thought. *Maybe that's one of the reasons why I like Jamie—because he's not like the rest of us.*

She sighed as she folded the letter, sealed it, and marked it Special Delivery. (She needed an answer fast!) She didn't feel any nearer to a solution than she had when she started writing to Amy. Putting the letter on the night table, she flicked off the light, scrunched down into her pillow, and stared at the darkness. Chess? Soccer? Mandy Harris? Who *was* Jamie Thompson anyway?

The next morning, Kate felt a little better. Amy would understand and set everything right. As she applied the last brush of blusher across her cheeks, Kate took a close look at herself in the mirror. She was usually vague and unconcerned when it came to her appearance. She knew she was nice-looking and had a knack for putting together great-looking outfits. But she took those things for granted;

they were just random elements that helped her feel confident—until now.

Now, as she looked at herself, she felt a twinge of doubt. *Aren't I his type?* She grimaced at herself as she brushed the tangles out of her hair. *What is his type anyway?* Does he have one? It can't be Mandy Harris. Kate would have heard if Jamie had dated Mandy, and up to now she hadn't heard about him dating anyone. Before Beth dismissed Jamie as too weird for her, she reported that he'd been seen riding the bus with Sally Anne Breed. Kate and Beth decided that that wasn't a sign of romantic interest on Jamie's part—more like exchanging secret survival tactics, since Sally Anne was also dumb enough (smart enough?) to be taking Mr. Guest's "Terror Through Words" class. Other than Sally Anne, Kate didn't know much about Jamie's friends—except those guys in the band. But she was planning to change that starting today.

She ticked off two important stops on her Jamie itinerary: the library and soccer practice. It wasn't that she didn't see him every day. After all, there was English first period, and they had gotten into the habit of going to The Tomb together for Basic IIA. They *never* sat together at lunch—he didn't seem interested in crossing over into Kate's "territory," and she wouldn't dream of leaving the security of it. She figured if she saw Jamie in a different setting, he might see her differently. *Sure Kate, the school library—real romantic.* She smiled at herself. In some ways the library was a better idea than "accidentally" running into him at soccer practice. At least she wasn't out of place in the library—what excuse could she invent for being at soccer? *I'll think of something, like hiding in the laundry truck that delivers the uniforms,* she laughed. She ran the brush through her hair one more time. *Maybe he doesn't like blondes.*

Kate looked down at the lavender and pink cotton sweater she bought for herself when she'd taken Connie to the Briarpatch for jeans. *This is the best I can do,* she thought as she strolled into the library. It was probably just as well that Adam Brainard had cornered her at her locker and Cal Brooks had insisted on ironing out some stuff about homecoming. This way the library would be the first time today that she'd talk to Jamie. And she had promised to return Connie's copy of *Superfudge.*

She spotted a couple of freshmen scribbling notes to each other at the first table in the room. A quick look around the rest of the library failed to produce Jamie. *Where is he? He's always here at this time.* Kate decided to return *Superfudge* and then kill some time at the card catalogue. Jamie was bound to turn up.

The student librarian looked up from her book and gave Kate a bored look. "Can I help you?"

"I have to return this." She pushed the book toward the girl, whom she knew only as a senior, not by name.

"Did you enjoy it, Kate?" the girl said with vague contempt. "Or was it a little too old for you?"

Kate wasn't surprised that the girl knew her name —everyone knew the Morris girls: first Amy, now Kate, and soon it would be Connie's turn. But she was surprised by her unfriendliness. "No, I didn't think it was too old," she politely answered the girl's sarcasm. "Not even when I read it five years ago." She paused. "I'm returning this for my little sister, Connie. Here's her card." She handed it to the librarian.

"Is that supplementary reading for the SAT's?" a familiar voice said behind her.

She turned around to see Jamie. "Where did you come from?" she asked a little too eagerly.

"I was skulking around the shelves looking for pretty girls, and a copy of *The Wind and the Rain*," he answered.

Kate had wanted to surprise him, and instead it was the other way around. She wondered if she'd ever have the upper hand with him. "The *pre-*SAT's," she corrected. "No, the book's my little sister's." She refused to feel dumb because she'd never heard of *The Wind and the Rain*. Instead, she glanced down at Jamie's empty hands and said, "Didn't find it?"

"No. Somebody else must have it out." He looked a little disappointed, which made him all the more appealing to Kate. She felt like running to a bookstore at that moment to get him a copy of the book. She'd tie it up with a nice blue ribbon and give it to him with her best smile. "I'll find something else." He brightened. "I did find a pretty girl."

"Here's your sister's card back," the librarian interrupted.

Kate turned to her and took the card absent-mindedly. "Thanks." *Why does he say stuff like that...about a pretty girl...when he doesn't ask me out?* She figured it wouldn't sound too retarded if she asked him a small question about his book. "Are you reading that for Mr. Guest?"

"The Wind and the Rain?" He sounded a little surprised. "No. It's one of my favorite books."

"Who wrote it?"

"P. J. Hilton. I really like it," he said with enthusiasm. "You should read it sometime."

Kate decided to get on firmer ground. Hilton's name sounded vaguely familiar to her—very vaguely, as a matter of fact. So she turned to something she knew a little better. "How is Mr. Guest's class?"

Jamie gave her a knowing look. "You were right about him. He's pretty terrifying, isn't he?" He didn't wait for her confirmation. "He's really tough, but he's very good. He forces you to think for yourself and think things through. It's challenging, but..." He stopped and said, as if he were talking to himself instead of Kate, "I'll be lucky if I pull a C-plus or B-minus in the class."

"Guest has to give some good grades. Not many, but a few. So you'll probably be one of the ones to luck out," she said enthusiastically.

Jamie ran his long fingers through his hair. Kate wondered what his hair felt like—it looked so soft and silky. "It won't be luck. That's for sure. Just sheer hard work, but I like it."

Kate's eyes lingered for a few seconds on Jamie's hair before returning to his blue-gray eyes. She was impressed with his determination. There were only a handful of kids who would stick out "Terror Through Words."

By now the two of them were getting nearer the

cafeteria, and Kate knew that meant they had to separate. She wished she could bring herself to sit somewhere else, but she couldn't. *Might as well end on an upbeat note.* "At least you can always count on Ollie for extra help with the class."

Jamie smiled. "Yeah. He's great, but I have to get him new glasses. He stepped on his old pair."

"I half-believe he does wear glasses," Kate said.

Jamie looked at her, his face a mask of mock disbelief. "Would I lie to you about my dog? Especially Ollie, who finished my French homework for me last night while I was asleep?"

Kate nudged his side. "You're something else," she said, meaning more than she could ever possibly say.

The two went through the cafeteria line together, then split for their separate tables.

Amy's such a peach, Kate thought as she spied the Special Delivery letter from her sister on the front-hall table a few days later.

"Must be something important," Mrs. Morris said as she passed from the den, glanced at the letter, and started for the front door. "I almost forgot." She stopped and turned. "Tell Connie I left the money for her United Way donation next to the sugar canister." She waved over her shoulder. "See you all in about an hour and a half. I promised Margie Reynolds I'd help her out at the League of Women Voters. Bye."

"Bye, Mom." Kate was already halfway up the stairs to her bedroom. She tossed her books on her desk and tore open Amy's letter as she bounced onto the bed.

Dear Kate:

Thanks so much for writing. I'm not Queen of Anything yet, but I've only been back a few weeks, so we'll see what happens. I can picture you devouring this letter looking for THE ANSWER about Jamie, so I'll tell you what I think. (I'm not checking off boxes, silly. I'm never too busy for you—especially when it comes to boys.)

Don't gasp when you read this, but I think Jamie sounds great. One of the best things about college is that you get to meet all different kinds of people. I don't think you should hold it against Jamie that he doesn't hang around with your crowd—even though you may find it hard to believe, not every super person at Hampstead is in the "in" group.

I remember how dippy we all thought the band members were, but one of the nicest guys in my music theory class was Jimmy Ortiz. You probably don't remember him (I barely did when I first ran into him), but he was in my year and played the trumpet in the band. I don't want to sound as if I'm preaching from a podium, but sometimes the "in" and "out" stuff can smother you a bit in high school. Just that whole cafeteria scene with the invisible "territories" makes me feel a little sad—and relieved to be here. Back to Jamie. You two sound as if you get along with each other, so why not ask *him* out instead of waiting in the wings? He'll probably be flattered. Any guy would love to go out with you. Why not ask him to the homecoming dance…the two of you would probably have a great time.

Have to go now—psych paper due tomorrow.
Love to all and keep me posted about Jamie.

Amy

PS. Sophomore year is even better than
freshman. I'm still skinny and Cece says hi
back.

Hugs,
A.

Kate reread the letter twice before she put it down.
Ask *him* out?! Unbelievable. Was Amy crazy?

Dear Kit:
Thanks so much for your answer (you didn't
sound preachy, just a little different). Guess
you're right about Jamie, but I can't can't can't
imagine me asking him to homecoming. I know
things are changing, but never never in my
absolute whole life have I had to ask a boy to
anything. Jamie *is* different, though...I'll let
you know what happens.

Hugs and kisses,
Kate

Chapter Five

On Saturday morning Kate's little sister woke her up to ask for a ride to the museum. Kate pulled the covers over her head as she slowly recalled the day before. *What a joke that was,* she thought as she unreeled the whole scene in her mind.

She had finished with cheerleading practice and had checked out the soccer practice schedule in the athletic office. The office secretary's question about "thinking of taking up soccer" should have been a sign that she wasn't going to pull this off. The secretary must have had eyes in the back of her head because Kate thought she was being fairly casual and unobtrusive in front of the bulletin board where the schedules were posted. She had probably taken too long finding the time when she knew Jamie would be going on or coming off the field.

She had carefully rehearsed her story: "Oh hi, Jamie—what a surprise," she would say casually when she bumped into him. It wouldn't be like the library scene, where he had spotted her and thrown her off-guard with *The Wind and the Rain.* Or worse, like the time she saw him with Mandy Harris. No, the soccer scene was better rehearsed. *Nothing could go wrong,* she had thought.

She had on her cheerleading uniform, and she'd fixed her hair with a red grosgrain bow that looked really cute with her outfit. Her cheeks were still flushed from all the practice exercises, and she was a little breathless from hurrying through the underground mazes that led to the field where the soccer team practiced.

Kate had slowed up as she neared her destination and repeated in her mind her excuse for being at soccer practice.

"What are you doing here?" Jamie would ask in his friendly, even manner.

Kate would laugh and grimace at the same time as she answered, "I'm doing an assignment for Comp IV about the poetry of sports, and I figured that everyone else would be doing football and basketball. So I decided to be different and do soccer."

She hadn't figured what Jamie's answer would be to that, so she would follow up with her big lie of the day: "I didn't know you were into soccer…" Then he'd take her hand and they'd live happily ever after.

But that wasn't the way it went at all. Kate remembered. Instead of "bumping into" Jamie, she had lingered around in the shadows off to the side looking in vain for him. *Where on earth could he possibly be? Did something happen to him? Why am I being such an unbelievable jerk staging this whole scene for a character who doesn't even bother to show up?* She had pulled the red bow from her hair and started back into the maze under the bleachers, angry and sad at the same time.

"Hi. What are you doing here?" Jamie had called. (The right opening words, Kate remembered.)

Kate was so startled by his familiar figure hurrying down the hall toward her—toward the practice field—that she was struck dumb. This wasn't the way it was supposed to go at all. And she also couldn't think of anything to say when she saw Jamie's smooth broad chest. He was in such a hurry that he was pulling on his jersey while he spoke to her. She longed to reach out, stop him, and touch the muscled skin and feel its warmth under her fingertips. But all she could do was stand bolted to the floor and say, "I...um...got lost on my way...um—"

"Sorry—I've got to go," Jamie cut her off. "I'll see you." He smiled as he rushed by her.

Even now Kate cringed when she remembered it. *Lost?* Thank heavens he was so late that he couldn't stick around to hear whatever else she might have come up with. It would have been too embarrassing; she might have—

"Does the red or blue look better with these?" Connie asked, interrupting Kate's mental replay of the disaster. "I like the red, but I wore it to the museum last week."

Kate shrugged her shoulders. "They both look fine with the jeans. And it doesn't really matter, does it, if you wear the same thing as the week before? The museum isn't a real high spot for fashion, is it, Connie?"

"No," she agreed. "But there's this really cute new guide there, and I wanted him to notice me." She escalated her enthusiasm. "He's so funny. Last week he explained the star show in the mini-planetarium to us in a voice that sounded like Donald Duck. He's really smart and he's so cute."

"You already said that," Kate replied. She'd never heard Connie so excited about a visit to the museum. Usually she ranked it a few steps above going to the dentist—a necessary part of growing up. "Does this dream guy have a name?"

Connie brightened. "Yes. Jamie. Jamie Thompson. He must go to Hampstead 'cause he doesn't seem that old."

Kate was stunned. *Jamie!* She had been picturing a lively thirty-year-old guide. Jamie had to be the very first guy from school who'd volunteered at the local museum for children. "Are you sure it's Thompson?" she asked Connie.

"I'm sure. I wouldn't make a mistake about him. He's so nice to us." She suggested helpfully, "I can find out if he goes to Hampstead and what year he's in. You'd really like him."

Kate froze. *That's all I need—to have my little sister quizzing Jamie on my behalf.* She answered firmly, but casually, "That's okay. I think I do know him. We have some classes together." She smoothed Connie's hair. "You better hustle, kid, or you're going to be late for your date with Jamie," she teased. "I'll be in the car." She would have given anything to see Jamie with the kids at the museum. *He really is adorable,* she said to herself.

She switched on the car ignition and was greeted by a blast of Weird Noise from the speakers. She lowered the volume and decided two things: 1) she'd give those tickets to Connie; after all, wasn't that what big sisters were for? (and besides, Jamie hadn't taken the bait when she mentioned them); and 2) she would definitely summon up the courage to ask Jamie to the homecoming. Anyone who could charm a bunch of squirmy eleven-year-olds at the museum really was a special—if a little off-the-wall—kind of guy. She would ask him first thing Monday morning before class.

It was a day when Kate was glad she lived within walking distance of school. Not too close, and just far enough now for her to make absolutely sure she was right about asking Jamie to homecoming. One part of her felt like a different person, some-one small and frightened, just because it was *she* who was doing the asking—not the accepting— to a school dance. Another part of her felt like regular old Kate—the easy, self-assured girl who saw something she wanted and decided to get it. The "it" in this case, however, she reminded herself, was an adorable, unpredictable boy who had shown some interest in her, but hadn't asked her out. But her confidence wasn't shaken as she ticked off a yes I ask him/no I don't chart in her mind.

The air was soft and warm, bathed in brilliant autumn sunshine that lighted Kate's hair a special golden color. She had spent extra time getting ready this morning: an extra smudge of gray eye pencil brought out the blue in her eyes, and she decided to wear her gray jeans and gray sneakers with one of her favorite turquoise sweaters which matched her eyes. She looked like a knockout.

She quickly went through the list of good/bad things about Jamie: *good*, he says I'm smart and pretty; *bad*, he hangs around with some really strange types; *good*, he's a jock; *bad*, he plays soccer; *good*, he's got one of the nicest smiles on one of the nicest faces I've ever seen; *bad*…she couldn't think of anything bad about him when it came to looks; *good*, he's smart; *bad*, he's almost too smart (chess? Mr. Guest's class?); *good*, he's fun. She decided to stop there. *He's fun and interesting. So why play some dumb game in my head!*

Kate knew what she was going to say and where she was going to say it. *Keep it casual and short. Meet him at his locker, ask him, and then walk with him to English. No big deal.* She smiled. She knew exactly where his locker was because she'd passed by it a couple of times in the afternoon hoping to "run into" him there. It was number 842, and she'd wondered as she'd passed by what was inside of it. Books? Pictures? Stuff?

As she drew nearer to school, she had some last twinges of doubt. She began to feel sorry for boys who had to do all the asking out. How did they feel when they got turned down? She felt a little relief: at least that was the thing she didn't think she'd have to worry about—getting turned down. She began to plan her outfit for the dance. She'd wear the burgundy velvet dress that Amy had lent her. Should she wear her hair up or down? Up would look really pretty with pink and burgundy ribbons wound through it, but Jamie would probably like it better down. And it would be easier for him to touch it—play with it afterwards—if it were down. They'd be the stars of the dance—she'd be responsible for the gym looking as great as it did, and Kev and Adam and Billy and Tim would ask her to dance, and she'd joke with Jamie about needing a dance card. But mostly she'd dance with him under the twinkling silver lights that looked like stars crowning her happiness.

A few "Hey, Kate's" snapped her out of her dreaming, and she looked down the hall toward Jamie's locker. He was fighting a losing battle with a big textbook that kept slipping off the shelf back into his hand.

He was still fumbling with it when Kate strolled up to him. "You look like you've got a rubber band between your hand and that book."

He turned and laughed. He never seemed surprised to see her, the way other boys did. He gave the book a last shove and quickly slammed his locker door. "There. Now it can't escape until it attacks me when I open the door later. That wouldn't make a bad movie—*The Attack of the Killer Textbook*." He paused to give it some consideration and started to walk.

Kate fell in step beside him. This wasn't exactly the way she'd planned it, and she felt as if she'd lost some advantage she imagined she'd have if they lingered by Jamie's locker.

"Not a bad idea, at all," he continued. "A boy comes home, puts his books on his desk, and slowly through the night they multiply until they become savage killers able to—"

"Jamie, I want to ask you something." Better to interrupt him now before he got too involved with the plot of *The Killer Textbooks*.

He turned and smiled at her. He looked so nice: today was a *Preppy Handbook*/Nike day, and he had on a plum-and-navy-striped rugby shirt.

55

"Sure," Jamie said. "What is it?"

Kate's tongue was paralyzed for a few seconds. She couldn't shape her words, but she took a quiet, deep breath and some of her confidence returned. "I was wondering if you'd like to go to the homecoming dance"—she paused—"with me?"

For once, Kate saw surprise flicker briefly across Jamie's face, but his smile never dimmed. "That's a really nice idea. I'm kind of surprised."

Kate was waiting for the "yes" word. Why wasn't he saying it? She began to feel her heart pounding.

Jamie said very sweetly, "Thanks an awful lot, but I can't." He was very polite and gentle. "It's nice of you to ask, though."

Kate's feet felt as if she were wearing fifty-pound weights in her shoes. *What am I supposed to say now?* She was waiting for him to explain that he couldn't go to the dance with her because he was going to be in Tibet that week. Or he'd be recovering from emergency surgery. Or even that he'd promised Mandy Harris that he'd play chess with her that night. But he didn't say any of those things. Just thanks, but no thanks. Kate knew she had to say something—even though she felt as if someone had just hit her in the head and stamped REJECT in big red letters across her forehead. She summoned up all the false cheer she could muster and said, "Thought you might like it." She caught her breath for a second but kept her smile intact. "Maybe another time."

"Sure," Jamie said in the same friendly voice he'd used to turn her down.

Kate felt as if her mouth was going to crack from keeping the brittle smile in place. She didn't have the heart to keep walking with Jamie—she actually wished right then that she didn't have a heart, because it ached so much. She snapped her fingers. "Gosh, I forgot. I left my copybook back in my locker," she lied. She waved at Jamie and turned quickly away. "See you later."

She stumbled back to her locker, fumbled with the lock and opened it—if only to have some place to hide her face for a minute. She wanted to crawl inside it and die. *Why* had he turned her down? There were at least three boys who would give anything to go to homecoming with her. Why did she have to like *him* anyway? And why was she dumb enough to ask him out? She felt like strangling Amy—if it hadn't been for her, she might not have gone ahead and done such a stupid thing. She knew it wasn't Amy's fault. Kate had asked Jamie out because *she* wanted to, because none of the rules seemed to apply to him. So she'd gone ahead and broken one of her own rules—never ask a guy out—and look what had happened.

She quickly brushed away some tears that had started down her cheeks. The class bell screamed a warning and she realized she was already late for class. She slammed her locker shut and ran on her leaden feet to Mrs. Griffith's class. She pushed her hurt deep down inside her, willed herself to smile, and vowed to tell all to Amy tonight.

After what had seemed like one of the longest days of her life, Kate dragged herself up to her room, hung the No Molestar/Do Not Disturb/That Means You sign on her doorknob, and retreated inside.

She buried her head in her pillow, and for a few minutes all she could hear was her own breathing, until deep sobs welled up from inside her. All day long she had replayed every encounter, every word with Jamie. Over and over—especially the turndown. Why hadn't he given her a reason? Then it wouldn't have hurt so much.

Muffin had been playing with some belts in the closet, but now she quietly leapt up on the pillow as if to comfort Kate. She reached out and stroked the cat's fur. Then she snuggled her head against Muffin's soft, warm body. She still felt miserable and *achy* inside, so she slowly sat up and reached for a pen and some paper. Muffin nestled in her lap while she wrote to Amy.

Dear Kit:

I feel so awful. (Sorry I'm not starting out with a cheery greeting, but...) I thought about everything you said about Jamie, so I decided to ask him to homecoming, and you know what... he turned me down. For no reason. It was horrible. I had to drag through the whole day pretending I didn't mind being an outcast. (I didn't tell anyone I was asking him, so no one knew—I hope.) I even had to pretend that everything was fine every time I ran into *him*!

I swear I will never ever be nice to him again. I know what I'll do. I'll act the way I did today around him—friendly, but kind of distant—sort of hard to get. (That's a laugh—look who's *really* hard to get!)

Oh, Kit, what can I do? He was so nice about it,

which made it worse for me. I wish I understood him, but I don't. I can barely stop crying. I hate him for making me like him! (No, I don't.) Please write.

Hope your life's happier than mine.

Hugs,
Kate

Chapter Six

Kate sat surrounded by Kev, Cal, Tim, Bonnie, and Janie at lunch. (Beth was two tables away "getting to know" Mike Collins better—mostly because he'd shot up four inches over the summer and had turned into a candidate for one of her new crushes.) The smile on Kate's face belied the ache she still felt around her heart. *No one* must find out about her asking—and being turned down by—Jamie. The humiliation would be unbearable. She thought that no one would find out, because an inner voice (the same one that told her Jamie wasn't absolutely the meanest boy in the world and must have a good reason for not being able/not wanting to go to homecoming with her) told her that Jamie wasn't the kind of guy who'd go around bragging how he'd turned Kate down.

"Kate, will you stop playing with your coleslaw," Kev said. "You act like you're playing food inspector for a day, counting how many shreds fit on your fork." He laughed at his little joke about "shreds."

Kate didn't seem to think his "joke" was very funny—nothing seemed funny or fun or just plain not sad to her. Still, she had to keep up her facade (she also figured that by acting happy on the outside, some of it might filter through to her insides). She smiled at Kev. "I think I'd make a good food inspector, but if it bothers you, I'll be glad to stop." She put her fork down with prim exaggeration, secretly relieved not to have to take another bite of anything. "What is it that you have to say that's so important?" she asked with her practiced, flirtatious grin.

Kev warmed to her attention. "I want to remind you that homecoming is only a few weeks off and I still don't know what the gym is supposed to look like."

"I thought we already decided that," Kate answered. "The rock posters: you know, the glow-in-the-dark ones."

"Yeah, yeah, I remember that part," Kev said, "but what I want to know is, what about the lights that Hardesty promised you?"

"Kev and I are clever, ingenious guys," Tim joined in, "but even we aren't expert electricians."

"You don't have to be." Kate was fiddling with her coleslaw again. She didn't want to look beyond the boundaries of her table for fear that she'd catch sight of Jamie in the distance. "Mr. Hardesty'll send some guys from the store to help."

"Boy, he certainly thinks you're great, doesn't he?" Tim said.

Kate just smiled back. She didn't know—or care—if Mr. Hardesty thought she was great. All she knew was that Jamie didn't think she was great enough, and for some reason he counted more than anyone else right now.

"That'll be fine," Kev said. "Tim and I will 'supervise' the lighting."

"Could we stop talking about the decorations for a few minutes?" Bonnie asked. "I want to know who everyone thinks will be elected Homecoming Queen." She paused. "And don't tell me what you guys think, because I already know you'll say 'Sheila Downey' because of her incredible body." She turned to Kate and Janie. "What do you think?"

Janie spoke up quickly: "Marcia Sherman, for sure. She's pretty and smart and nice." She scrunched her face up in a fake grimace. "She's perfect. I think I hate her."

Kate was looking at her fork. She'd heard Bonnie's question and didn't really feel like answering it. She didn't want to talk about homecoming—she didn't even want to go to it, but she knew she had to. It would look really bad if she didn't. Kate sometimes felt that her name was synonymous with school spirit. Up until a few days ago, she was proud of that—now it felt like a burden. Still, she had to act as if homecoming were as important to her now as it was before Jamie's turndown. "Janie's right. It probably will be Marcia."

"Okay, that's settled," Bonnie stated emphatically. "Now, what about the Handmaidens?"

Kate rolled her eyes. "They haven't been called that for forty years."

"I know, but that does describe them," Bonnie answered. "Better than 'Assistant Homecoming Queens.'"

"They're the Belles," Janie said. "And I know

someone who's bound to be elected." She looked at Kate.

Kate wasn't really surprised. Not that she was one hundred percent certain about being elected a Belle, but it was something that she more than half expected. "We'll see" was all she said.

"Have you decided on your outfit?" Janie gushed.

"Janie, they haven't even had elections yet," Kate said half seriously. She could hear Tim and Kev talking about the Vikings out of her left ear, and for a split second wondered why they were discussing history. Then she realized they were talking football. *Does Jamie ever talk about football?* she wondered. Then an image of him pulling his shirt over his naked chest before going onto the soccer field flashed across her mind, and she quickly blinked it away. *Why does he have to have such a nice broad chest anyway?*

Bonnie looked at her watch. "Don't know about you guys, but I've gotta run. Just for the record, though"—she smiled at Kate—"you're sure to be a Belle."

"Thanks, Bonnie," Kate said as she picked up her tray.

"I'll get that for you," Kev offered. And before Kate could say anything, he snatched her tray and plunked it on top of his as if the two "belonged" together.

"Thanks, Kev," Kate smiled. "Let me know anytime I can do anything for you." She instantly felt like biting her tongue because Kev needed so little encouragement.

He flashed her a pseudo-evil grin. "That right, Kate? I'll take you up on that, but what I want from you"—he paused, glancing both ways as if he were checking to make sure he and Kate were the only two people in the cafeteria—"can't be discussed in public."

Kate laughed at his exaggerated flirtatiousness. "You *are* silly," she said as she walked off with Bonnie and Janie.

"Are you going to go to homecoming with him?" Janie asked.

Kate's smile slipped a bit. "I don't know who I'm going with." She restored her smile. "Do you think the lead singer of Victory is free?"

Bonnie smiled. "You know something, Kate, if there's one girl in our class who could get a date with him, it would be you."

"Oh sure," Kate said sarcastically, "in a minute. Why stop with him? What about the cover guy on *Rolling Stone*?"

"I'm serious," Bonnie insisted. "You can get a date with anybody you want."

Kate was glad the three girls were at the cafeteria exit, about to go their separate ways. *If Bonnie only knew the truth.* She kept her smile, in spite of her thoughts, and waved to her friends. "See you all at practice. Don't be late."

"Bye, Kate," Bonnie and Janie said brightly.

Out of the corner of her eye Kate saw the last person in the world she felt like running into and he was heading her way with Brian Winter. She willed herself to speak to him—politely but coolly. "Hi, Jamie." She gave him a tight smile. "Hi, Brian." Before they had a chance to answer, she glided two steps ahead of them and tried to pretend she was a princess followed by two knights.

"Where are you hurrying to?" Jamie asked.

"I'm not hurrying anywhere." She exaggerated the word "hurrying" so that it sounded a little silly—at least to her and, she hoped, to Jamie. "Actually, I'm going to the library."

"Me too," Jamie said enthusiastically. He sounded as if he enjoyed her company and wanted to be with her—even in the library.

Kate was baffled. *He doesn't sound like someone who just turned me down for a BIG DATE only a few days ago. Maybe it wasn't* me *he didn't like—just the homecoming.* She had maintained her pace a couple of steps ahead of Jamie and Brian. "By all means, feel free to accompany me," she said a little too archly. *It's okay to walk like a princess, dummy, but don't push it too far. You sound like the Queen Mother.*

"Did you hear that King Oliver record that BJ got?" Brian asked Jamie. "It's super—a great mellow sound."

Kate was now glad to be two steps ahead because that way she didn't really have to join in the conversation. Which was just as well, since it didn't sound to her as if Brian had addressed his question to her anyway. Which was more than okay, since she didn't know who King Oliver was. She knew every hit name in music (she thought), but who was King Oliver? He couldn't be very big if she hadn't heard of him.

Jamie answered quickly, "No. When did he get it? I love King Oliver. Is it part of that Smithsonian record collection?"

"I'm not sure," Brian answered. "You've got to hear it, though; you'll flip. He does 'Good Time

Mama' like nobody else."

"I bet it's great," Jamie said. "Do you like blues, Kate?" he asked. Brian hadn't really bothered to include her in the conversation.

Kate shrugged her shoulders and said casually, "Sure." She was glad that the library was a few feet ahead. She didn't feel like going through a lecture about King Oliver that would make her feel dumb the way the dance card thing had done. Why did Jamie have to know about stuff she'd never even heard of?

"Catch you later, JT," Brian said in a friendly voice to Jamie. "Bye, Kate." He sounded shy when he spoke to her.

"Bye, Brian," she answered, thinking those were about the fourth or fifth words she'd ever spoken to him. The band was really considered strictly off-limits for anyone who was "in."

"Catch ya, Bri," Jamie called after his friend. He turned to Kate. "He knows so much about so many different kinds of music—it's phenomenal. I swear you could ask him anything and he'd have the answer."

Kate wasn't really impressed—except at how impressed Jamie was. She knew as much as she cared to about music. At least she thought she did. Anyway, she was determined to keep some kind of lid on her enthusiasm around Jamie, so all she said was "He's in the band, so he should know a lot, right?" She tried to sound as casual as possible, which wasn't too hard right now because she really didn't care about a band member, even if he was a friend of Jamie's.

"Right," Jamie agreed, "but most people don't

know half of what he does."

Kate was bored with music. *No,* she corrected herself, *I hate it that Jamie and I get along even though he's interested in stuff I've never heard of.* She fumbled for a book in the quilted satchel she carried her school things in. "It's nice he's so interested," she said vaguely.

She was so distracted by Jamie's presence that she realized too late the book she had absentmindedly pulled out to return to the library was one by P. J. Hilton. *Rats and double rats,* she said to herself, *now he'll know I was hanging on every word when he was going on about P. J. Hilton last time we were in the library together.* She decided to make the best of her slip-up and take the initiative. She held the book out—almost for Jamie's approval. "You were right about P. J. Hilton; I just loved this," she said, looking at the copy of *Beyond the Hill* in her hand.

Jamie looked at the book blankly and his face seemed puzzled. "You liked that?"

"Yes. She's such a good writer," Kate beamed. "I can't wait to read *The Wind and the Rain.*"

"Gosh, I'm surprised you liked that." Jamie nodded toward the book in her hand. "I thought it was pretty..." He didn't seem to want to finish the rest of his sentence.

"Pretty what?" Kate asked. She couldn't figure out what the problem was. He had told her that P. J. Hilton was one of his favorite writers, so she had raced back to the library, checked out the first one of her books she could find, and then stayed up super-late for two nights in a row reading *Beyond the Hill.* Now Jamie was looking at it as if she vere holding a dead mouse in her hand.

Jamie ruffled his hair. "Pretty boring, I guess." He shook his head. "*The Wind and the Rain* is the *only* book of Hilton's I like."

Kate felt better and worse about Jamie's remark: better, because she, too, thought *Beyond the Hill* was a little boring (even if it was well written); and worse, because she felt as if she'd made a fool of herself all over again in front of smart, cute, *totally unpredictable* Jamie Thompson. She decided the best way to salvage the situation was to be positive, cool, and upbeat. "Then I guess I really *must* read *The Wind and the Rain*. The 'only' book for you is the 'only' book for me," she said brightly. She felt like strangling and hugging Jamie all at once. Would the day ever come that he didn't surprise her? *Probably not,* she thought.

"What else have you been reading?" he whispered as they sat down next to each other at one of the library tables.

Your mind, she wished she could say. She figured she might as well be truthful and nonchalant. "Just the latest bodice-ripper," she smiled.

"Say that again," he laughed.

"A bodice-ripper." Had she at last found something he hadn't heard of? "You know, those eight-hundred-page romances with titles like *Sweet Savage Passion* and *Flames of Love*."

"Can't say I've read any," he said, still curious. "Where did you get that nickname?"

"Bodice-ripper?" she answered. "That's because someone is always trying to tear off or unlace or remove by force the breathless heroine's bodice."

"Tsk, tsk," Jamie teased. "A young girl like you

reading books like that."

Kate nudged him gently in the ribs. "Get real Thompson," she smiled, "*everyone* reads them.. except boys, of course. They're off-limits to you."

"Why? Because I'd learn the hidden secrets of a young girl's heart?" he joked.

A pang went through Kate. He was teasing and this whole conversation was in fun, but when she heard him say "hidden secrets," it reminded her of how much she was hiding from him. All her thoughts and feelings and longings—he knew nothing about them. And she wanted to keep it that way—for now. "The biggest secret you'd learn in one of those books is how complicated eighteenth-century underwear was," she said, looking at him with a half smile that made her eyes light up. "That's not something you're *really* interested in, is it?"

He shook his head. "Bodice-ripper," he repeated softly and laughed again. "You're really funny Kate."

Chapter Seven

Dear Kate:

I wanted to call you after I got your letter, but my funds are really low. Besides, this way I can say some things I might not over the phone.

To start with, your world hasn't come to an end because Jamie turned you down. (He really *is* different, isn't he?) I can't imagine why he did—it may be as simple as that he hates formal dances. Or that he's doing something else that night. I know you'll find it hard to believe, but for some people, especially someone like Jamie (at least the way you've described him), homecoming isn't the MAIN EVENT of the school year.

You're probably feeling a little better by now (I hope, I hope), so listen to big sister Amy's advice for the week (or for the next ten minutes, whichever is easier to take). As awful as it was at the time, the turndown may not have been the worst thing for you. (I have my Polly Preacher hat on again.) At least Jamie knows you're definitely interested in him, which gives you the freedom/choice/option to back off a little if you like. (If you can figure that out without

71

rereading it twice, you're invited to join me in Psychology 201, one of my favorite courses.) Seriously, don't shut Jamie out of your life entirely—he sounds so nice. Even you said he turned you down in a nice way.

Meanwhile, I know you'll have to turn down at least two boys before you decide who's the lucky one to take you to homecoming. You have so many friends. Which reminds me, have you been elected a Belle yet? You're an absolute sure thing.

What are you going to wear? Don't say a "black dress and black veil" because Jamie turned you down. Look absolutely smashing (not hard for you) and have a great time. And if Jamie's at the dance (which I somehow doubt, based on my Psych 201 instinct), BE NICE to him—not *too* nice, just nice enough. Show him you can have a good time with or without him—and *mean* it, even if it's something you have to work on. I know he's really got you confused/heartbroken/happysad/madglad all at the same time, but try and keep your perspective. (I really do sound like Polly Preacher, especially since I'm dying to get to know a guy better who sits a couple of rows ahead of me in psych. You should see him— he looks like he just stepped off a magazine cover ... really. Later for him—this letter's supposed to be for you.)

I really do feel for you. The situation will get better—I promise. Actually, it probably already has improved. Check one:

☐ Yes, a tiny bit.

☐ No, I've decided to become a nun.

☐ I'm not going to speak to him for at least two weeks. He made me feel like a frump.

☐ Jamie who?? I can't even remember whom you're talking about.

Got to go now. Cece and I are going to a Phi Delta party. The members are interesting—sort of a combination of *Animal House* mixed in with *Revenge of the Nerds* and *Geniuses on Parade.* (I made up the last title, but you get the idea.)

Write and tell me about the dance—and everything else. I *know* you're going to be a Belle.

Hugs,
Amy

Kate put the letter down (after rereading it, especially the freedom/choice/option part about Jamie). Did Amy mean that being rejected by the boy of your dreams actually was good? How? She was free all right, free to go with anyone *except* Jamie. He'd placed himself off-limits, at least for the dance. Well, she'd act a little more off-limits too. She congratulated herself for doing a pretty good job of it—except when she felt dumb about that whole P. J. Hilton thing in the library.

There was a knock on her door, and before she could answer Connie burst in with Muffin cradled in her arms.

"You look like you're wearing a fur muff, Connie." Kate fixed an evil grin on her face. "Do you think that when Muffin dies we should make her into a muff?"

Connie looked stricken, and Kate was instantly sorry that she was taking out some of her frustration about Jamie on her little sister.

"That is absolutely the most horrible, cruel thing I've ever heard." Connie nuzzled her face into the cat's fur. "You didn't hear mean, awful Kate say that, did you, Kittykins?" she said in baby talk to the cat.

Muffin leapt out of Connie's arms and in one graceful swoop landed on Kate's bed. She crept across the comforter and rubbed against Kate's knee. Kate petted her and said, "I guess she still doesn't understand English."

"Lucky for her," Connie said with a little quiver puckering her chin.

Kate looked up and said sweetly to her little sister, "I'm sorry, Connie. It was just a dumb joke." She patted the bed near Muffin's tail. "Sit down and tell Kate all."

Connie walked cautiously toward the bed and then bounced down hard. "Yeeee, I love to do that," she giggled. Muffin looked up, startled, and pounced to the safety of Kate's night table.

"Someday, you'll be sorry when you break this and have to pay two thousand four hundred weeks' allowance to have it repaired," Kate warned half seriously.

"I know," Connie dismissed Kate's comment. "Anyway, first things first. They repaired the ceiling pipes in the school library, so we can use it again." She smiled at her sister. "You don't have to raid the Hampstead Senior High stacks for poor, deprived me anymore. May I have my card back?"

Kate didn't tell her little sister that she was be-

74

ginning to get a little tired of the senior librarian's snide remarks about what babyish taste she had in books—especially for a junior in the Honor Society. She gestured toward her quilted satchel. "Sure. It's in the little pocket on the inside top."

Connie opened the satchel carefully. "Do you think Mom would make one of these for me? It's so pretty."

"You have to ask her," Kate said. "But you know how long it takes her to do one of these, and she's bound to remember that your canvas bag got dragged in the mud when you had the fight with Tommy McGuire."

"We weren't fighting." Connie looked indignant. "We were kidding around."

"Whatever," Kate said. "But what about the time you ripped it on your school locker?"

Connie answered defensively, "I can't help it if JHS 41 is one of the oldest, most decrepit heaps of a building in town. And that the lockers are so bent out of shape and battered that they practically have claws on them." She fished her card out and gently flipped the top back, giving the bag another fond look. "Oh well," she sighed. "Guess it could be worse. I could be hauling my stuff back and forth in a grocery store bag—the way Peter Talbot does." She rolled her eyes and wrinkled her face in disgust. "Dork city."

Kate was getting a little impatient. She didn't feel like discussing bookbags all afternoon. "Listen, I've got a lot of stuff to go over before dinner. Okay?"

"Sure," Connie said agreeably and started for the door. "Oh, I almost forgot." She stopped and turned to Kate with a big smile on her face. "That cute guide at the museum, Jamie, said he knows you."

Kate felt like strangling her little sister. *Why, why did she have to brag or show off or whatever and mention that she was my younger sister? I don't want him to think I'm spying on him.* She caught herself in mid thought. *Why on earth would he think that?* She collected herself. "I *told* you, Connie," she said in a pleasant voice that had undertones of menace in it, "that I probably *did* know him. I'm sure he's not at the museum to yammer about everyone's brothers and sisters."

Connie didn't appear to pick up the menace in her sister's voice. "I don't know. He seemed kind of glad that I was your sister. Said you're really nice." She shrugged her shoulders and waved her library card in the air. "Thanks for this." She opened the bedroom door.

Kate hated the idea of Connie's talking about her with Jamie and vice versa. It broke the wall of silence she'd built up around her real feelings for him. No one except Amy was supposed to connect Kate and Jamie—not even through something as tenuous as a little sister's friendliness with her museum guide. Kate called after her sister: "Do me a favor and don't make friends for me, pleeeeze. Or I'll make you a bookbag so special that you'll be the only eleven-year-old at school carrying her stuff in a big animal-shaped pocketbook."

"Give me a break, Kate," Connie said. "I don't know what the big deal is, just 'cause I told Jamie you were my sister." She closed the door behind her, cutting off any answer Kate might have had.

Kate picked up Muffin and scratched her fur until she was purring softly in her lap. *I wonder how Jamie's face looked when he told Connie he thought I was nice? I wonder if he said any more than that—besides the "nice" part? Or how his voice sounded when he was talking about me?* She gave herself a final command. *Stop tormenting yourself about him.* She smiled to herself. *Torment yourself with homework instead.*

"You look really beautiful, Kate," Billy Hutton said in a dreamy, far-off voice.

"Thanks, Billy," Kate said. She felt like telling him not to sound as if he were in the presence of a movie star. "You look nice too."

He beamed at her in silence, confirming for her that it was not a good idea to be going to homecoming with Billy. In fact, it was probably a big mistake to have turned down Kev and Tim to go with Billy, even if he was the sweetest. And pretty cute. And they'd been friends forever. But that's all she wanted to be—a friend of Billy's, and nothing more. His eyes spoke more than friendship.

Kate was glad her parents had gone to the movies, because she would have been a little embarrassed having them see her and Billy go off to the dance together. They liked Billy a lot—a whole lot, which made it all the worse.

Billy held out a cellophane box to Kate. "These are for you. The guys told me that Belles are supposed to wear white roses."

She took the box from him. *The guys.* She pictured Billy quietly bragging to Adam and Kev and Tim about how *he* was going with Kate. To homecoming. With Kate, the prettiest Belle of all. She opened the box and the sweet fragrance of roses breathed through the air. "They're really beautiful, Billy." She quickly fixed them on her dress and looked up at him. "Really," she assured him.

"That dress looks beautiful," Billy said. "You look beautiful."

Kate took his arm. "You already told me that once," she teased. "It's just me—same old Kate." She tried to sound casual, as if to remind him of their days on the jungle gym together, in order to defuse his crush. "Let's go or we'll be late."

"Sure," he said amiably, leading her out the front door as if she were a rare and delicate flower that was blooming for only one night.

Beth and Bonnie rushed up as Kate and Billy walked into the Hampstead gym. "Hi, Billy. Doesn't everything look great?" the two girls gushed. "You guys did a fabulous job." They turned to Kate: "You look gorgeous." Then back to Billy: "Can we steal her for a minute? We promise to bring her right back."

"Oh...sure," Billy said. "I'll meet you near the stage."

"Great. See you in a minute," Kate said as her two friends spirited her off to the ladies' room. "Thanks, guys. I don't know what I'm going to do about Billy tonight," Kate sighed. "I swear he'll suggest we elope before the dance is over."

"He is cute enough to elope with." Beth grinned as she pushed open the door to the ladies' room and a cloud of giggles and chatter floated out.

"He's a little young to 'settle down,'" Bonnie

said. She turned to Kate. "That dress is *super*. Why didn't you tell me you were wearing it?"

"I wasn't sure what I was going to wear," Kate said. Which was the truth. She had tried on twelve different outfits ranging from an emerald-green satin blouse and knickers (the saleswoman had insisted that she *must* try them on) to a black taffeta strapless dress. Finally, she settled on the blush-pink dress with puffy sleeves and a deep-pink sash that encircled her waist. She had put her hair up and nestled a small organza bow in it. A few curls fell onto her long neck, and some stray wisps grazed her cheeks. She looked radiant.

"Turn around, let me see the back," Beth said.

Kate twirled obediently and the skirt floated like petals around her knees.

"Oh, I love it," Bonnie said. "All the other Belles are wearing long dresses..."

"They are?" A faint furrow creased Kate's forehead, then disappeared. "I thought we could wear long or short...long looks too much like a prom dress instead of homecoming."

"You look perfect," Beth confirmed. "All you have to worry about is outshining the Homecoming Queen."

"And eloping with Billy," Bonnie laughed.

Kate shook her head. "He's so sweet, but he's like a brother. I've known him forever."

"He must be super-proud to be with you, and he looks so cute," Beth said.

Kate sighed to herself. *He does act so proud to be with me.* She glanced at her reflection in the mirror. She had tried to look her very best—not for Billy—but for Jamie. She half hoped he'd be here tonight, although she didn't really think she could bear seeing him dance with another girl, holding her, instead of Kate, in his arms.

"He's cute," Kate said vaguely. But she was thinking about Jamie, not Billy.

"Come on, you all," Bonnie urged. "We've got to get back. You know how Tim hates it when his date isn't available every minute."

The three girls drifted back into the gym. Kate found Billy. "When you were in the bathroom, they announced that all the Belles should go backstage and get ready for the presentation," he said.

"What about you?" she asked.

"They told us to meet you at the bottom of the stage, as you come down." He smiled warmly at her. "I'll be there, waiting for you. You know, Kate, I—"

She cut him off. She didn't want to hear some pledge of love or undying friendship that Billy might say. Instead, she wanted to be up onstage, not so that she'd be the center of attention, but so that she could get a better look at the crowd and see if Jamie was among them. Even now—especially now—she couldn't get him totally out of her mind. Kate squeezed Billy's arm gently. "I'll see you in a little while. Wish me luck." She hurried backstage.

"Hi, Kate," Janie Sherry greeted her.

"I'm really nervous," Kate admitted. "I'll probably trip or something."

"No way," Janie assured her.

Then Mr. Winston, the principal, announced the presentation of the Homecoming Queen and her Belles. One by one the girls walked slowly out onstage until they formed a semicircle of six for the Queen.

Kate smiled at the applause. She was glad she was the second girl out—it gave her more time to check out the audience. But she couldn't see beyond the glare of the stagelights. The applause and whistles came from behind the curtain of darkness that shrouded all the kids looking up at the stage. As hard as she tried, she couldn't make out *any* faces, much less Jamie's.

The presentation ceremony lasted fifteen minutes, and when it was over, Kate glided off the stage and down the steps to where Billy was waiting for her. "You were the prettiest girl up there," he beamed.

The band played "Let Me Love You Tonight," and Billy put his hand under Kate's elbow and guided her onto the dance floor. He gingerly put his arm around her, and took her hand and began to dance slowly to the music. He drew her closer, and Kate regretted once again that she'd said yes to Billy.

As they danced around, Kate kept sneaking peeks over Billy's shoulder, hoping to see Jamie, but she hadn't spotted him yet. Maybe Amy was right; maybe the reason he'd turned Kate down was because he didn't like homecomings—or dances—or both. She hoped he wasn't here, because he wasn't *her* date; but she also hoped he was, so that he could see her in the dress she had picked out partly with him in mind.

Then she saw him. He was standing by the punch

bowl laughing with Mandy Harris. Had he turned her down for Mandy? She couldn't believe it.

Kate knew she had to talk to Jamie so she said, "Billy, the lights onstage were so hot. I'm kind of thirsty. Could we get some punch?"

"Oh sure." He quickly stepped back but held on to her hand. "I'll get some for you if you want to sit down."

"No. No," she replied too quickly. "Let's both go."

She kept her eye on Jamie as if to fix him in one spot with her gaze, but he didn't seem to be going anywhere anyway. He was still talking to Mandy, who was wearing, Kate noticed with a squeak of satisfaction, a droopy brown velvet dress that looked like something borrowed from her grandmother's closet. Jamie had on a tweed jacket and gray pants, which wasn't exactly the right outfit for the evening, but it didn't matter. He looked adorable.

"Hi, Jamie," Kate said with the coolest smile she could manage. She felt like dancing every dance with him, but she'd never let him know. "Having a good time?"

Jamie looked at Mandy and grinned in an odd way. "It's hard to say. I'm here because Mandy crucified me in our last chess match and she made me promise to show up here as a punishment for losing." He sounded as if he were teasing and telling the truth at the same time.

"Hi, Mandy," Billy said. "Excuse me while I get some of those cups behind you." By accident, Billy had edged Mandy to the side, leaving Kate and Jamie facing each other.

"You looked pretty up on the stage," Jamie said.

Kate felt like saying, If I'm so pretty, how come you're here with Mandy in her droopy brown dress? "Thanks. Somehow I didn't expect to see you here." Did that sound too conceited? Too bad, she *had* to say it.

"I'm a little surprised to be here myself," he said with his easy smile. "But Mandy's too valuable a chess partner to lose." He didn't say any more than that.

Kate believed him—almost. One thing she was sure of, though: Jamie was always full of surprises.

Billy turned around holding two cups of punch. He looked so proud and happy to be with Kate as he handed her a cup. He held his up and said, "A toast to the real Queen of Homecoming." His eyes shone.

Kate felt a little embarrassed by Billy's obvious devotion to her, and she didn't dare check out Jamie's reaction to it. But she decided to capture some of Jamie's attention by flirting...with Billy. She smiled warmly back at her date and said, "I swear, Billy, I'd be Queen of Everything if it were up to you."

"You deserve to be," Billy said in a voice that sounded as if he thought Kate was the only other person in the room.

"What's going on?" Mandy Harris turned back to the group and gave Jamie a cup of punch. She didn't appear to be too interested in what was happening.

Jamie half smiled. "We're holding a brief testimonial here for Kate."

"Oh," Mandy said blankly, and absentmindedly

sipped her punch. She surveyed the decorations and the couples on the dance floor. "This is better than I thought it would be."

"You know, Mandy, you're right—as usual," Jamie said. "It is better." He looked at Kate and raised his cup to her.

She flickered her eyes away from his and turned a warm look on Billy. "To a happy night." She hoped her words would make Jamie just a little jealous.

Chapter Eight

A few days after homecoming, Beth rushed up to Kate before class. "You've got to see the story about homecoming in the *Clarion*—there are two pictures of you." She thrust the paper into Kate's hands. "Here, look—you can give it back to me later. I'm meeting Mike Collins."

Kate skimmed over the story—it was the same old stuff about it being one of the most fabulous nights of the year for Hampstead students. The memories. The magic. The fun. Kate thought they must reprint the same story year after year and just change the names and dates. She looked at the photos scattered throughout the feature: there was one of her—and the rest of the Belles assembled onstage. Where was the other photo of her? Her eyes stopped at a slightly out-of-focus shot of her and Billy and Jamie at the punch table. Mandy must have been cropped from the shot. Kate couldn't remember anyone taking her picture then, and as she looked closely, she realized it was just a candid. She was between Jamie and Billy: the photo was clear enough to capture Billy's worshipful expression. Kate was smiling at him with her head tilted slightly away from Jamie.

Thank heaven for that. All she needed was a photograph certifying how she really felt about Jamie. *No*, she thought, *this is fine; we're all smiling, but the picture reveals nothing*. The only true thing about it was the caption: "An advance look at next year's Queen???"

Kate had some time before Mrs. Griffith's class, so she lounged against her locker and browsed through the rest of the paper. Everything was pretty predictable: editorials on students' rights and responsibilities; some record and music video reviews (everyone loved the Nylons); sports stuff and student writing. Kate was only half reading the student essay on Poe when she saw the name James E. Thompson under a short poem called "Beauty."

She looked at the name over and over, almost caressing it with her eyes. All her feelings about Jamie welled up when she saw his name—his formal name—in print. She read the poem slowly, once, twice, a third time.

Beauty

No one else but you holds it in your
Heart. Through everything else it
Lights from within, and
Glows on into the long shadows
Of tomorrow.

James E. Thompson

She wasn't sure what the poem meant, but she was pretty sure that somehow it was a secret message to her, a way for Jamie to express what he really thought and felt. It *was* about her, wasn't it? *Kate, get serious*—interrupted her voice of reality. *Is he really the kind of guy who writes public love notes? Come on, you're trying too hard.* Kate folded the paper—carefully—because she didn't want to crease the poem or the picture of her and Jamie, since she intended to clip both the first chance she got.

Kate had been dying to write Amy about homecoming. She'd gotten another copy of the *Clarion* so that she could send the Jamie photo and poem to her sister. She sat cross-legged on the bed, shooed Muffin away when she tried to dance around on the newspaper, and carefully clipped the poem and picture.

Dear Kit:

Here's the update. (Isn't it great the way I launch right into my problems, affairs, events, etc., without asking you how you are?)

Homecoming was really nice—we did the gym so it would look as much like a rock video as possible: posters, special lights. Yours truly was responsible for the theme (pretty much—I'm so modest, aren't I?).

I bought this great dress that looked perfect— you have to promise to borrow it sometime. The picture doesn't really do it justice, but take a good look at the picture because THERE HE IS in living black and white: Mr. Heartthrob. (Billy's on the left, but I didn't have to tell you that, since we've all known him since practically before he was born.) Isn't he cute? Jamie, I mean...

The phone on the desk rang again and again. "Doesn't anyone else live here?" Kate said as she reached across the desk to answer it.

"Hello," she said impatiently.

"Hi, it's Billy."

Kate grimaced at the phone and thought, *Why, oh why, did I say yes when he asked me to homecoming? Now he thinks we're more than just school buddies.* But she couldn't be mean to Billy. He'd been too nice for too long. "Hey, what's happening with you?" she said in an offhand, friendly way. "Keeping in shape for Saturday's game?"

"That's what I was calling about."

"What?" Kate teased. "You want me to drop my pom-poms for the game and be starting quarterback against Central?"

Billy sighed. "No, I wanted to ask you if you'd like to go to the victory celebration after the game."

Kate had to refuse gently. "What makes you think you're going to win—for sure?"

"They're a bunch of losers at Central," Billy said. "You know that. Their record is oh and six. There's no way they can beat us." He paused a bit. "So what do you say? Can you come to the celebration?" His voice sounded so sure, full of more certainty than Kate had ever heard from Billy— at least when it came to her.

"I'm sorry, Billy, I can't." She tried to sound regretful, but not too regretful. She also thought it sounded better if she didn't offer him some excuse.

There was silence on Billy's end of the phone. "How come you can't go?" He sounded so disappointed—all the certainty had drained out of his voice.

"I just can't," Kate said firmly. "I have a million things to do."

"Oh...uh, okay...I guess I'll see you tomorrow." His voice started to sound hopeful again. "I'll save you a place at lunch."

"I'll have to see," she said finally. She didn't think it was fair to encourage him at all. Although it didn't take much to encourage him. "I've got to go now—I've got heaps to do. Thanks for calling. Bye."

His soft voice sounded like an echo drifting into the distance. "Yeah. Okay. Bye."

Kate went back to her letter eagerly.

...he really is a dream, don't you think? I have to explain what he was doing there. What I mean is I'll tell you what *I* think and then you tell me what it means—because it may make the turndown not so awful.

He was there with...don't drop the letter... Mandy Harris. He said she'd beaten him at chess and asked him to take her to homecoming. Should I believe him? Do you believe him? Would he bother to lie? He doesn't seem to be the type. I really do think it was a last-minute thing and that he hadn't planned to come at all, and that's why he turned me down. Right? Or do I win the Pollyanna medal for the week?

Anyway, I figure...

The telephone rang unanswered again. "They probably don't bother sometimes because they figure it's for me," she muttered as she scrambled across her desk to pick up the phone. "Hello."

"Kate?" a familiar voice asked. "It's Jamie."

Please, please God, don't let him be calling up just to chat or fill me in on how Ollie's progressing with his homework (as cute as that is). I can't stand the tension. Kate willed her emotions to calm down for a minute. "Hi. How've you been?" *That sounds calm enough,* she thought, *calm enough to be* boring.

"Since you passed me by in the hall this afternoon without saying hi, I've been okay." He sounded half hurt, half teasing.

Kate remembered that. She'd been late for physics and was running down the hall with Kev. She'd seen Jamie strolling along in his official Zzekes and Zzopes slow walk, and she really didn't have time to stop. And since she didn't, she figured she might as well play it cool and not say hello. "I'm sorry. I was super-late for class." She tried not to sound apologetic, just matter-of-fact.

"Listen, I don't want to keep you on," he said, "and besides, Ollie's paw hurts, so *I* have to do most of the homework tonight."

"Sure, I understand." But she didn't. *What does he want? To tell me I didn't say hello to him?* She was *not* going to talk about Ollie now. This was the "new" Kate, friendly but distant.

"I wanted to know if you could go to a band rehearsal with me tomorrow."

He was asking her out (sort of). She yearned to spend heaps of time with him. But why did he have to ask her to a band rehearsal? And why did he wait until practically the last minute? Boys didn't do that. The words "Yes, I'd love to" were forming in her mouth, but she bit them back. *After all, isn't one of the reasons he's asking me out because I've drawn away from him a little bit? Acted as if he were one of many guys who were interesting at Hampstead?* She was pretty sure that was the reason, so she decided he'd be more interested in her if she didn't fall all over him because of one invitation—and to a band rehearsal too! She reshaped her answer, and replied as casually as possible. "Gee, I'm sorry, Jamie. I'm busy tomorrow. But maybe another time," she said brightly.

"That's too bad," he said. "You'd like rehearsal."

"Sure," she lied. *The only thing I'd like about it is you sitting next to me. Better keep up the elusive image.* "Thanks for asking, though. I've got to go, but I'll see you tomorrow. I promise I'll say hello."

"Okay. Talk to you soon," he said agreeably. Kate could hear a bark on Jamie's end of the phone before she hung up.

Flash—flash—flash. You're not going to believe who just called—HIM. The main topic of this letter. He asked me to go to a band rehearsal with him tomorrow. You'll never guess what I did...don't tear the letter up. I said *no.* It isn't as if I wanted to, I just figured that he'd become more interested in me the less interested I seemed in him. I hope I'm not wrong. Oh Lord, what if I am and he *never* asks me out again?

We didn't talk long—part of my "aloof" strategy. And I didn't give him a reason either. That should keep him guessing, yes? At least I hope. Oh, Kit, I'm so excited. I'll stop talking about myself for the next thirty seconds.

How was the Phi Delta party? They sounded weird but fun. Actually I thought the blond guy in *Revenge of the Nerds* was kind of cute. That reminds me, did I tell you that Bonnie is giving a Nerds party? Everyone's supposed to come dressed as their favorite kind of nerd. Could be funny—or really dumb. Come to think of it— why should I want to dress up like a nerd for a party? I'm sorry. I've started talking about myself again. Can't wait till you're home for the holidays. Please save twenty minutes for a "Jamie" conference with me. Muffin keeps trying to paw this letter—maybe she can read and is trying to say hello. I know she misses you— but not half as much as I do.

Please give me a Psych 201 evaluation of the hard-to-get strategy. I have to go now, but I'll continue this tomorrow night.

Jack's was packed with kids from Hampstead. It was *the* hangout, and the front booths were un-officially reserved for the "in" crowd—that is, Kate and her friends.

Mike and Tim had picked her up, and now the three of them joined Bonnie, Kev, and Beth. As she slid into the booth, Kate realized she'd been coming here about two nights a week for the past three years—ever since eighth grade.

"Hi, guys," Beth said. "Did you hear what Kev heard Sally telling Rob?"

"What?" Bonnie asked. "Is she—"

Kate cut her off with a tired voice: "That she's absolutely breaking up with him, once and for all."

"Yeah, but this time—" Beth said breathlessly.

"I know," Kate finished the sentence for Beth. "This time it's for real." She sighed. "They've broken up 'for real' every six weeks for the past two years."

"Guess what Central's planning to do during halftime this weekend?" Kev asked.

"I don't know. What?" Bonnie asked.

"They're doing this flash card thing, spelling out the names of the team," he answered enthusiastically.

Kate fiddled with a straw that someone had left on the table. "They do that almost every game," she said. "I swear, Central must do that flash card stuff so all the students can learn how to spell."

The conversation went on: from who liked the Spikes better than Weird Noise, to how boring shop was for Adam and Kev, to whether or not Mrs. Griffith shaved her mustache (a student debate for years). Kate tuned out the conversation, as well as the Howling Dog music bouncing off the walls of Jack's. She began to wonder why she'd never seen Jamie here, but it wasn't too hard to figure out. A clubby-type hangout wasn't what he seemed to like. He always seemed so happy just doing the things he enjoyed.

She also began to feel like a real jerk for having turned him down. Had she cut off her nose to spite her face? When she turned back to the conversation at the table, Kev was saying, "Come on, Adam, Mrs. Griffith doesn't."

"Wise up, Kev," Adam said with a laugh. "They should have her doing those razor commercials instead of the baseball jock."

"You're terrible," Bonnie laughed.

When Kate got home, the first thing she did was retrieve the letter to Amy from her desk drawer, where she'd hidden it under some papers. She re-read it and added some final paragraphs.

As promised, here's more of "The Letter." Nothing much to say—went to Jack's with everyone (Bonnie, Beth, Adam, Kev)—you know, the usual cast of characters. It was kind of a drag —some jokes about Mrs. Griffith's mustache. You know, the same old stuff.

I feel like a dumb, dumb jerk for not having gone with Jamie, but why did he have to ask me out the night before the rehearsal? He acts as if I should be ready to go whenever he wants (not really—I don't think it really occurs to him). I wish he'd act as if he really, really wanted to be with me.

The only way I think I can make that happen is by keeping up the hard-to-get act. That way, when he asks me out, it'll *mean* something and won't be just a last-minute thing. I'm confused. Give me some Psych 201 info.

Got to go.

Hugs,
Kate

Chapter Nine

Dear Kate:

Sorry I didn't get back to you sooner—stuff has been piling up in heaps and heaps: quizzes, papers, oral presentations. I think my professors are having a secret contest to see who can assign the most work in the shortest space of time. Yikes, I can't wait for the Christmas holidays (if I'm alive by then).

I don't know what kind of Psych 201 information would help right now about Jamie. A description from *Alice in Wonderland* would fit him better—"curiouser and curiouser." What I mean is he sounds like someone who gets more interesting as time goes on. Even Connie mentioned him in a letter she wrote—told me about the "cute museum guide."

I know how hurt you were by his homecoming turndown. (Before I forget, thanks for the pictures. You looked adorable and he is cute—Jamie, I mean. I've always thought Billy was cute.) But you *like* Jamie—you wouldn't have been so hurt if you didn't like him a lot. That, and the surprise factor—he's probably one of the few guys who would turn down an invitation from you. I'm not so sure that playing hard to get is such a great idea—especially with him. He sounds like a guy who really doesn't respond to games. He probably asked you out now because he wanted to wait a while—get to know you before he did decide to spend time with just you alone.

Jamie sounds awfully mature for his age, and different in a good way (something that you mentioned before). Given who you are—one of the "stars" at Hampstead—some boys might ask you out just to make themselves look good. You know—the "guess who *I'm* taking out next Friday" stuff. And that's kind of insulting to you when you think about it.

It sounds as if Jamie is asking you out for the right reasons—because you're smart and sweet and fun to be with, not because you're pretty (although that's nice too), or popular, or belong to the "right" crowd. Think it over before you keep up the hard-to-get game. Anyway, it sounds as if *he* has a patent on it—the big difference is, it isn't a game with him. It's really the way he is—a guy who belongs pretty much to himself. You know, he sounds like a good subject for one of my psych papers. He sounds as if he's oblivious (that's a college word for "just doesn't care about") to other people's opinions.

This letter has gone on too long—I know you want to hear more about cute JT, but I've got to hand in a paper tomorrow on "The Landscape of the Soul: Emerson vs. Poe." (Can you hardly wait to get to college after hearing that? It's about Ralph Waldo Emerson's and Edgar Allan Poe's different approaches to life and art.) I don't know what to say at all, even though I've done tons of research.

One last thought—don't play around too much with Jamie's feelings. He sounds sensitive and nice. And another last thing: you have a lot of other nice friends and you're involved in lots of action as it is. Don't forget about them—Jamie isn't the main activity at Hampstead.

Hugs and kisses,
Amy

PS. Billy H. is so sweet—just thought I'd mention it, although I think you overwhelm him.

Kate reread Amy's letter. She agreed with some of it—Jamie being cute, and different in a nice way—and disagreed with other parts. (Was he really someone who didn't play games? Didn't everyone play games at one time or another?) Oh well, she'd play the Jamie situation by ear, even if it was frustrating sometimes.

She loved the expression "the Jamie situation" because it made him sound almost manageable, as if she could categorize parts of his personality and create different files about him: *Looks; Brains; Personality; Pet Peeves; Hobbies* (that file would be huge); *Girlfriends* (that file should have one name in it—Katherine Miranda Morris). As she learned new things about Jamie, she'd slot them into the appropriate file until she had a JT file cabinet that contained everything there was to know about him. Then there would be no surprises. But Kate wasn't sure she'd like a Jamie without surprises—wasn't that part of his appeal? She smiled to herself at the image of Jamie categorized and filed away—

that would be like trying to bottle a rainbow or file a ray of sunshine. It couldn't be done. *And what's more,* she thought, *it shouldn't be done, especially with Jamie.* She thought of him as a beautiful proud horse, free-spirited and untamed. No, you could never control someone like that.

But doubts still nagged at her. You could put a bridle on a horse and it didn't hurt him—so why couldn't she try to get Jamie to do things the way she was used to? It wouldn't hurt anybody, would it? And then you could make the horse go where you wanted—not *all* the time, just sometimes. Is that what she wanted to do with Jamie? She wasn't so sure it was fair to bridle a wild horse—even if it could be done. *Forget it,* she told herself. *File cabinets and bridles are dumb. Just do what strikes you best when the time comes.*

As they had for more times than Kate could remember, she and Jamie walked from Mrs. Griffith's class over to The Tomb. This morning she had planned to go over by herself, just so that Jamie wouldn't *always* think that she was *always* ready to fall in step with him. She had collected her books together quickly and had rushed out of the room (as discreetly as possible) so that she'd be pretty far ahead of Jamie, but she hadn't gone far down the hall when she heard his voice.

"Are you practicing for the walking race at the Winter Carnival?" he teased.

She turned around and gave him a little smile. He was still a few steps behind her, and she looked down at his long legs, thinking, *No wonder he goes so far so fast...those legs could go anywhere.* She noticed that today was a Nike day for Jamie and his fast feet. He had on his jacket that said "Late Night" across the back and a blue oxford cloth shirt with jeans. *He is adorable,* she thought.

"You know there's no such thing as a walking race at the festival," she said.

"If there were, you'd win it hands down."

"You mean 'feet down,' don't you?"

"I stand corrected." He made a gallant gesture, saluting her elaborately.

"Where do you suppose that expression originated?"

"Which? 'Hands down' or 'stand corrected'?"

Kate shrugged her shoulders. "I don't know, either one." She didn't really care all that much, which she was glad about because it helped her act kind of indifferent toward Jamie.

"I'll find out and let you know tomorrow," he said helpfully.

"It's okay. I won't die if I don't find out."

He smiled. "I won't either, but I'm curious about things like that—origins of words and expressions. I think it's really interesting because it sort of combines history with English."

Kate thought that Jamie was so special just because of things like that. He'd probably come back tomorrow or whenever, his eyes alive with the new information about "hands down" and "stand corrected." But all she said to him now was "Sounds interesting. Good luck."

They walked in silence for a couple of minutes toward the dark halls of The Tomb. Kate didn't mind it when she and Jamie didn't say anything to each other. He wasn't like other boys who sometimes were silent; they were nervous or shy. He was just relaxed and talked mostly when he had something to say. Kate looked down at her feet, 'and in an imperceptible switch fell exactly into step with him. Her feet looked tiny and delicate in their plain black skimmers next to his. She liked the way they looked—the two pairs of feet, walking side by side. *Partners,* she thought.

"I wanted to ask you something," Jamie said. "I was wondering if you'd like to walk home together today."

Kate almost stopped in her tracks. Had she heard him right? Was he really asking her to do something with him again? She didn't know how to answer, so she stalled for time. "I didn't know you lived near us," she lied. She'd known his address since the first day of school, when Beth had told her that his parents had rented a house on Miller Avenue.

"It's not near, exactly, but it's on the way," he said. "We live at 220 Miller Avenue—it's kind of far from school, but I don't mind the walk because you go through some interesting neighborhoods on the way."

Kate wondered how he knew where she lived and that it was on the way to his house. Had he been asking about her? Had he looked it up in the yearbook? She savored an image of him taking the yearbook down from the shelf in the library, turning the pages till he came to her picture...reading all the quotes and activities under her photo. Had he done that? She wished with all her heart that he had. Why not ask him? "How did you know where I live?" she said curiously.

"Brian Winter told me."

The romantic image of Jamie poring over Kate's yearbook photo faded in her mind. *How does Brian Winter know my address? Oh, it doesn't matter. That isn't the main problem right now. What do I say? Yes or no? Why couldn't he have asked me on a date date, not just a walk home from school. Although that would be awfully nice, with the air so crisp and the brilliant autumn sunlight shooting through the turning leaves.*

If I say yes, he might think I'm available whenever he wants. If I say no, it might make him like me more—and ask me out on a real date next time. But she wanted to walk home with him so much. She flipped a coin in her head: one side had a big YES on it, the other side, NO. The coin came spinning to rest with the NO side up. She turned to him. "Gee, that's a nice idea, but today is when I tutor at the community center," she lied, hoping he wouldn't remember that tomorrow was her real day there. *Why didn't I make up a more glamorous lie? Oh well, at least this reminds Jamie that I do a lot of things that don't involve him.*

"That's too bad," Jamie said. "Maybe another time."

The two of them walked the rest of the way—which was only about a minute and a half—in silence. Kate kept going over the consequences of what she'd just done. *It was okay to say no—after all, it's a same-day invitation, and it's only for a walk home. It wasn't as if he asked me for a real date.* A pang of doubt struck her. *I've turned him down twice now. Will he ever ask me out again?* She looked down at her feet and noticed that she'd fallen out of step with Jamie.

Kate's answer came a few weeks later when she and Jamie were walking toward the library. She sometimes wondered why Beth or Bonnie didn't comment on the time that Kate and Jamie spent together—even if it was only walking to and from classes. They probably didn't even notice, since Jamie wasn't in their crowd. And if they did notice, they probably figured that Jamie was just another boy who had a crush on Kate. Just another guy who'd be happy to walk with her anywhere. Bonnie and Beth might think that Kate was just being nice to a guy who didn't stand a chance of getting any closer to her than a walk through the Hampstead halls. If they only knew.

"Do you believe the results of the election?" Jamie asked.

Kate thought he was talking about the rotating seat in the Student Council that had recently been filled. "I think Billy Hutton is a good choice."

Jamie laughed. "Not for Congressman from the Ninth District." He shook his head. "I'm not talking about the Hampstead election—I'm talking about the congressional race. I spent a lot of time working for Patterson. I can't believe he didn't win."

"Sorry, I was so myopic that my vision didn't extend beyond the hallowed halls of Hampstead," she said with exaggerated precision and haughtiness.

"It's really a shame—Patterson's such a good guy," Jamie said.

Kate didn't know what to say about the election. It was something she caught snippets of on the six o'clock news. "Well, at least the right man won in Billy's case." She was genuinely glad for him.

"Yes, I guess so," Jamie said abstractedly. His face brightened. "I know how you can help cheer me up. Come with me to the Mozart concert at Town Hall tonight. It'll be beautiful." He looked so happy. "It's three hours long—you'll love it."

Kate was happy and sad at the same time. Mozart —for *three* whole hours? She wasn't sure she could listen to anyone for that long. And why did Jamie always ask her at the last minute? Guys usually asked her out *days* in advance. Maybe it was the spontaneous side of his nature. Still, this *was* a real date—a concert—with him sitting next to her the whole time. She couldn't answer him right away—she needed to think about it. "What time does it get out?" she asked.

"Probably around eleven o'clock."

"That's kind of late for a week night—I'm going to have to check with my parents." *Check with myself is more like it. Should I say yes even if it's Mozart and the last minute? Or is it better if I say no? Then Jamie will understand how to do things the way I want—at least for our first date, which means making the invitation not sound like some kind of afterthought.* "Listen, I'll call you later and let you know."

Chapter Ten

Beep. Beep. Beep. Kate punched the last digits of Jamie's phone number. One ring. Two rings. She took a deep breath, ready to greet him when he answered.

It was four-thirty—it hadn't taken Kate too long to decide that she'd go out with Jamie, even if it was Mozart for three hours. She had finally realized that her hard-to-get game wasn't what attracted him at all. A little voice had whispered to Kate all the way home from school. Every time she said, "It's not a formal, ask-me-out-three-days-ahead thing," the little voice said, "Right. But it *is* a will-you-be-with-me-tonight thing. So what if you didn't get an engraved invitation? You did get an invitation." To which Kate said with an inner sigh, "Yes, but...Mozart? Three hours? When will we get to talk?" And the little voice said, "It wouldn't be Jamie if it weren't Mozart. That's one of the reasons you *like* him, because he's different from everyone else. You'll get a chance to talk." Then Kate said, "But, Mozart..." And the little voice said, "Look. You want to go out with him more than anything in the whole world. Right?" And Kate smiled to herself and nodded imperceptibly as she pictured Jamie in her mind. "Yes. I do." And the voice answered, "So what are we even bothering to discuss this for?"

There really wasn't a huge decision to make. True, she wished that Jamie had asked her to do something else—and had given her a few more days' notice the way other boys would. The words trailed off in her mind. He wasn't like other boys. But tonight she'd bring out the side of him that was more like her and her friends.

She was standing by the side of her bed with the phone cradled on her shoulder listening to the third ring, then the fourth. Where was he anyway? She started to shift the phone from her right ear to her left and considered sitting down, but reminded herself that she'd feel more in charge if she remained standing. When the phone was in "mid-ear" a woman's voice answered. "Hello."

Oh no, not his mother. And she sounded out of breath. Kate had been sure that Jamie would be home, sitting patiently by the phone, his hand poised over the receiver ready for her answer. Why was his mother ruining the scenario? "Uh, hi," Kate said brightly. "Is Jamie there, please?" She decided to be mysterious and not give her name right away.

"I don't think so," the voice replied. "I just got in myself, and I'm sure he would have answered it. This is his mother." Before Kate could say anything, Mrs. Thompson offered, "I'll double-check, though," and clattered the phone down.

Did they live in some forty-two-room house where Jamie couldn't hear the phones ringing while he wrote poetry, or whatever? Or did they have only one phone, and if you weren't near it, you couldn't hear it? Why wasn't Jamie near it anyway? Why hadn't he anxiously been waiting for her? Somehow Kate couldn't even be annoyed at him, just puzzled—as usual.

After what seemed like forever, Mrs. Thompson returned, picked up the phone, dropped it, and picked it up again. She laughed. "Sorry, I was trying to take off an earring and pick up the phone at the same time. Can't do both, I guess."

Kate acknowledged this with a little laugh. Jamie's mother sounded nice. Relaxed and friendly.

"My wandering boy doesn't seem to be around, but I know he'll be home in a little while because he's going out later," she said.

"Yes, I know," Kate answered. "That's why I'm calling—because he asked me out." *Why am I telling her this? Why don't I just leave my name and hang up?* The little voice supplied the answer: "Because you want Mrs. Thompson to know how urgent this call is and somehow tell her 'wandering boy' to call absolutely the very first minute that he shows his adorable face at home."

"Oh, I see," Mrs. Thompson answered. "May I leave your name for him?"

"Yes. It's Kate Morris," she said. "Do you have any idea where he is?" *Oh great—that makes it sound as if his mother should dispatch a rescue team immediately to locate "wandering boy Thompson." Why can't I just shut up and hang up?*

Mrs. Thompson sighed, but Kate sensed a smile through her answer. "You know him; he could be any one of a dozen places. But we're having an early dinner because of the concert."

Kate was warmed by Mrs. Thompson's acting as if the two women knew Jamie so well that nothing he did should really surprise them. But she was also panicked by Mrs. Thompson's mention of the concert: Jamie—even Jamie—wouldn't bring his parents along, would he? She took a silent deep breath (might as well know now) and asked, "Are you going too?" A nervy question, but a necessary one.

Mrs. Thompson laughed. "Oh no, dear. Of course not. It's just that we always try to have dinner together." She laughed a soft laugh. "No. Jamie is the only Mozart fan in this family."

Kate felt enormous relief. Her confidence swelled within her. Everything was back on course again. "Well, would you tell him I called and ask him to call when he gets in?"

"Fine. I'll tell him."

Both of them hung up.

Kate stepped over to her closet. She had been tempted to leave the message "Yes, I'm going with him tonight," but decided that that would be one of the super-nerdiest things she'd ever done in her life. No, let Jamie call her to find out "the verdict." Meanwhile, she'd put together an outfit that Jamie would never forget. She was going to be very organized about this, she thought, as she pulled three sweaters and four skirts from her closet.

First, she pulled on the red angora with the black ribbon threaded through the neckline and matched it with her favorite, one and only, black leather miniskirt. She appraised herself critically in the mirror. *No, too disco looking*, she decided and took off the outfit.

Next she put on a black V-necked sweater with a royal blue knit skirt. She fastened a necklace of black and crystal around her neck. She sighed at her image in the mirror. No, it was okay for Weird Noise, but not Mozart. She started to unhook the necklace when the phone rang. She leapt across the room and had her hand on the receiver after one full ring. It took all her willpower to wait one more ring before she picked it up.

"Hello."

"Hi, it's Jamie," he said with a smile in his voice. "Sorry I wasn't here when you called. I was over at Patterson headquarters helping to clean things up. Boy, there's nothing worse than a candidate's headquarters after he's lost an election."

Kate wondered how many people would be thoughtful enough—loyal enough—to stick with someone even in defeat. "That was nice of you to go there," she said. "I bet a lot of other volunteers weren't there."

Jamie chuckled. "You know, you're right. But it's the least I can do."

"And since you said you were depressed about Patterson losing, I've agreed to cheer you up by going to the concert," Kate said brightly.

"Great," Jamie said enthusiastically. "You'll love it."

Kate didn't dare correct him; Jamie was one thing to love, Mozart was another. "It'll be fun," she said truthfully.

"I know. Listen, I'll pick you up about six-thirty, okay?" he asked.

Kate was confused. Six-thirty, when the concert was at eight? Was he planning *not* to eat with his family? Was he planning to grab a snack with her instead? She certainly wasn't going to ask him about his dinner responsibilities with his family, so all she said was "Sure. That's fine. I'll see you then." She shrugged as she hung up the phone.

Every time she thought she knew what was going on with Jamie, Kate found herself puzzled. She unfastened the black necklace and took off the sweater and skirt. Seeing herself in her lace camisole and pants gave Kate an idea. *It's Mozart. Classical. Dressy. Right?* She wished she had the time and the money to call Amy right now, tell her about the date, and ask for some advice about clothes. But now that Jamie was picking her up an hour earlier than she expected, Kate figured she'd better hustle to look great and *not* be late.

She went back to her closet and fumbled around in the far right corner. Finally, she pulled a plastic garment bag from between some other dresses. *Please, don't be wrinkled,* she prayed as she unzipped the bag and pulled out a black and white dress that was one of her favorites. She smiled at the dress with admiration and relief as she took it off its velvet hanger. No wrinkles in sight. Just a delicate white lace top and black silk taffeta skirt.

Kate quickly pulled the dress over her head, congratulating herself as she did so. *This is perfect —it looks like a skirt and blouse, but it's dressy enough for a concert.* Her head popped into view and she admired the outfit once more in the mirror.

The neckline was scalloped with the delicate embroidered lace, and the short sleeves were slightly puffed at the shoulders. The tight waist had a velvet belt above the skirt that bloomed like a

110

beautiful black flower around her knees. Kate pulled black silk pumps with tiny heels from the floor of her closet and decided that all she needed to make the outfit complete were sheer black stockings and a string of pearls. She turned around to view herself over her shoulder. Satisfied that she'd made the right decision, she unzipped the dress and placed it carefully on her bed while she went into the bathroom.

After her shower, Kate wiped the steam off the mirror, toweled her wet hair, and started to put on her makeup—something that she knew how to do expertly. Sometimes she felt like offering to help the department-store makeup "artists," who, she felt, never knew that less could be more. You didn't have to put makeup on with a trowel to achieve the best look. She dabbed some rosy beige foundation across her face, then applied some creamy rose blush to her cheeks. She powdered her long lashes to make them thicker, then brushed on gray eye shadow and stroked some darker-gray eye pencil across her lids before applying black mascara. After putting some translucent powder over her whole face, Kate finished with some powder blusher across her cheekbones. Not too much of anything. Just enough to look…as pretty as possible for Jamie.

Kate checked the clock on her night table—five after six. She blew dry her hair, pulled a lock of it off to one side, and fastened it with a black and white comb. Her regimen was interrupted by her mother.

"Ka-ate, what are you doing about dinner?" she called.

Kate opened her bedroom door while she continued brushing her hair. "I'm not doing anything. I mean, I'm having something with Jamie."

"When?" Mrs. Morris was a fanatic about missed meals. Sometimes she acted as if a law should be passed about her children *never* missing a meal.

"Later," Kate answered, not exactly sure when "later" would be.

"Okay, but make sure you have something," Mrs. Morris said in a semi-stern voice.

"O-kay," Kate agreed as she shut the bedroom door. Muffin had slithered in before the door was completely closed and rubbed softly against Kate's bare leg. She leaned down and scratched the cat's neck through her thick fur. "I'm actually going out with him—do you believe it?" Muffin replied by arching her back once more against Kate's leg, yawning, and leaping onto the bed, somehow avoiding the dress.

Kate smiled. "Oh, what do you know anyway?" She finished her hair, put on some black pantyhose, carefully stepped into the dress, and zipped it up. As she was fastening the belt, she heard the doorbell ring. She glanced frantically at the clock —six twenty-five. Leave it to Jamie to be early. Kate took a last look at herself in the mirror, seized the little black clutch bag she'd prepared, and went down to meet Jamie. He wasn't someone to keep waiting.

Kate heart sank when she saw Jamie. Not that he didn't look cute—he did. It was just that they definitely didn't match. He had on a navy blue rugby shirt with a white collar and jeans. He did have on a navy and red tweed sports jacket, but no tie—no hint of anything "dressed up." And there was Kate looking gorgeous...and dressy. Definitely dressy. Too dressy. Suicidally dressy. Why was he dressed like that? Why was she dressed like this? *Where have I gone wrong with this guy?*

"Hi—you look beautiful," he said. For a minute, his smile made Kate forget her outfit, and the expression on Jamie's face made her feel as if the two were a perfect match—no matter what they were wearing. Then she snapped back to reality.

"Thanks," she laughed a little nervously. She gestured at her dress. "I—I think I should change."

"Why?" he reassured her. "You look great. Doesn't matter what you wear."

Just then Connie came in. "Oh, Kate, you look beautiful." Her eyes shone with admiration for her older sister. She turned to Jamie. "Hi," she greeted him a little shyly.

"Hi," Jamie said and softly tousled Connie's hair. "Am I going to see you on Saturday?"

Connie looked at him with amazement. "Of course. I wouldn't miss it for anything."

A flicker of jealousy went through Kate. She envied the time that Connie and Jamie had at the children's museum. Kate's little voice whispered to her: "Will you puh-leeze give me a break! It's *you* who's going out on the date with him."

Jamie turned to Kate. "We'd better get going if we're going to be on time."

Connie took the cue and exited.

"Sure," Kate agreed, and shut her mind to any possibility of changing her outfit. She got her black dressy coat from the front hall closet—and wished she could keep it on all night so she wouldn't look quite so different from Jamie. Then her thoughts brightened. *Maybe* he's *the only one who's dressed this way. Maybe everyone else will be dressed like me.*

Kate preceded Jamie out the front door and waited for him on the walk. She wondered where his car was. As he joined her, she fell in step beside him and decided to ask. "Did you park around the corner?"

He turned the collar of his jacket up so that his hair waved over it here and there. He looked at Kate with a faintly puzzled expression on his face. "Park?" He paused for a few seconds. "Oh, you mean a car. I don't have one," he said matter-of-factly.

Kate smiled and wondered what was next. She didn't actually mind not riding in his car (which didn't exist anyway), but she hadn't yet figured out how they were getting to Town Hall. "We're not *walking* to the concert, are we?" she said with a twinkle.

Jamie laughed. "No, I thought we could take the bus. It stops right in front of Town Hall."

The bus? Of course, the bus. Even though most kids at Hampstead wouldn't be caught dead on the bus, it didn't seem to matter to Jamie. "Sure," Kate said. And added truthfully, "It'll be different." She was glad her dressy black coat didn't look too dressy. *The bus,* she repeated silently to herself.

"I'll bet you don't ride the bus much, do you?" Jamie acknowledged.

Kate shrugged. Why should she feel that there was something wrong with *not* riding the bus all the time? "A lot of the people I know have cars," she admitted.

"You don't," Jamie said.

Kate liked it that he knew something about her she hadn't expected him to. "Well, no. But I can walk to school...and hitch rides anywhere else."

"I know. I've seen some of the cars lining up for you."

"They don't 'line up,'" Kate laughed. "It's just that—"

"Just that everyone wants to be with Kate." He smiled at her. "Including me," he added softly.

Kate wanted to snuggle up to him after that, but she knew that she didn't have the nerve. Instead, she looked down at Jamie's feet. Tonight was neither hightops nor Nikes—it was brown loafers, worn but polished. She made an invisible change with her feet and fell into step with Jamie.

The trip with Jamie had been an adventure. The two sat in the back of the half-empty bus and talked and laughed for the half-hour ride. Kate even forgot what she was wearing as the two chatted on about school (they both agreed that physics was not fabulous) and music (Jamie's favorite music, besides Mozart, was Klondike; Kate's was the Spikes) and movies (they both wondered who really liked *Slasher VII Returns*) and everything. It seemed only a few minutes between the time they boarded the bus and the time it pulled up to Town Hall.

Jamie got off first and held the door for Kate. "Age before beauty," he said.

Kate never heard anyone but her father say that, but still it sounded nice coming from Jamie. "You're not so old."

"Do you expect me to say you're not so beautiful?" He grinned. "It would be a lie anyway." The way he said it wasn't the way other boys did—as if they wanted something in return for the compliment. Or as if they were expected to say it. No, Jamie sounded natural about Kate's looks, and more interested in her thoughts than anything else.

So much of the conversation on the bus had been answering *his* questions. What do you think about this? How do you feel about that? But you don't really believe that, do you? He seemed to want to know more about her than he already did. So far, Kate's plan about drawing out the "real" Jamie hadn't gone quite the way she'd imagined, and she was beginning to wonder if her "plan" was that important anymore. She was having too much fun.

"Let's wait outside and let everyone else go in," Jamie said, taking Kate's hand and leading her to the wrought-iron fence that encircled Town Hall.

"Okay. That way I can see if I'll win a prize for being the most overdressed girl at the concert." Kate felt so relaxed by now that she could joke about her outfit.

Jamie laughed. "Doesn't matter what you wear." He was still holding her hand. He opened his hand and looked at hers. "But it does matter how cold your hand is." He tucked her hand, still in his, inside the pocket of his jacket. "There. That should help." He hugged her hand and then looked around at her other hand and gestured toward it. "Why

116

don't you put that in your pocket to keep warm."

Kate smiled at him. She hadn't even noticed whether or not her hand was cold. She felt a glow all over. "Whatever you want," she said teasingly, and slipped her hand into the warmth of her pocket.

The crowd filing into Town Hall was a mixture of young and old, singles and couples, casual and well-dressed. But no one was "dressed up" in the Kate sense of the word. "Looks like I will win a prize after all." She shrugged.

"You'd win a prize anywhere, no matter what," Jamie said. "Do you feel like going in?"

"Not really," Kate answered truthfully—to her own horror. She hadn't meant to be quite so candid, but Jamie had that effect on her.

"Still not convinced about the concert?" he asked.

"I didn't say that," she corrected with exaggerated emphasis. "I only meant I wouldn't mind staying out here a little longer."

Jamie gave her a playful nudge. "I promise you won't be bored. There's an old saying: 'When God smiled, it became the music of Mozart.'"

Kate was touched by Jamie's enthusiasm—and breadth of knowledge. "That's lovely. Where did you hear that?"

He seemed a little embarrassed and shrugged his shoulders. "I don't know. Somewhere." He took his hand and hers out of his pocket and led her into the hall. "Come on. You'll see."

The two of them sat down on the plush velvet seats of the old hall. Even though their seats were on the aisle, there wasn't a lot of room and Kate was forced to sit semi-sideways so that her left thigh brushed Jamie's. He didn't seem to mind and neither did she. So far, the concert was more than okay and the music hadn't even started.

When it did, it was everything Jamie had promised. The orchestra began with (Kate checked her program) "Piano Concerto No. 21 in C Major." The liquid notes floated in silver and gold clouds through the air, raining down a lush harmony of notes. Kate loved the music; it set her to dreaming about Jamie even as she listened. She thought about how he was so interested in different things, how he was so smart and funny, and...well, *everything*. She felt as if the music was swirling around the two of them—bringing them closer together. She couldn't believe it when the concerto was over and everyone began to clap. She checked her watch (for the first time) and saw that the orchestra had been playing for forty minutes. She excitedly joined in the applause. (Not for the first time during the piece. After the first movement, she had thought it was all over and began to clap. To her horror, she realized that her hands were the only ones breaking the silence of the hall. She looked at Jamie and grimaced. He smiled back and whispered, "I told you you'd like it." He didn't act embarrassed or awkward, or any of the things someone else might have been.)

At intermission Jamie stood up. "Well?" He looked at her expectantly.

"I loved it. I really did." Kate couldn't believe her own words, but they were true. The music— and being with Jamie—had made her feel warm and safe...as if she was in the right place with the right person at the right time. Everything fit.

Jamie took her hand. "I knew I could count on you," he said.

"What do you mean?"

"I knew you'd understand it all." He gestured toward the members of the orchestra who were still exiting the stage. "You're special." He took a slight breath. "And smart and curious." He looked at her as if she understood everything and everyone, including him.

She squeezed his hand. "Thank you," she said softly.

The rest of the concert was enchanting. It was mostly piano solos. The first, "Rondo in A Minor," reminded Kate of cool water in the moonlight. It was so languid and peaceful that for a few minutes she rested her head against Jamie's shoulder.

When it was all over, Kate felt as if she were awakening from a dream. She never thought she'd like—much less *love*—an evening like this. But she had enjoyed every minute of it. She realized with a smile that Jamie was bringing out the real Kate—not the other way around, as she'd planned.

Jamie put his arm around her shoulder as they walked up the aisle. "Well, *querida*, I'm glad you liked it."

Kate wished her Spanish was better. She didn't know exactly what "querida" meant, but she knew it was good. She snuck a look at her watch, hoping it wouldn't be too late. Ten-twenty. Oh, why did it have to be a school night? She knew that she and Jamie had to go right home—especially with the long bus ride ahead of them. *Well, at least we have that.*

"I caught you sneaking a look at the time,"

Jamie grinned. "I've got to get home too and see if Ollie's gotten all my homework done."

"I wasn't 'sneaking'—not really," she protested with a smile. "I was just hoping we had more time."

"Me too," he agreed, and added, "Next time."

Kate had assumed there would be a "next time" just because *this* time had been so special and it wasn't even all over. There was still good night. "Okay" was all she said.

The two waited in the clear, cold starlight for the bus. Kate began to shiver. (Her dressy dress wasn't very warm at all. Neither was her dressy coat.) Jamie stood in back of her and wrapped his arms around her shoulders, warming her with his body. She wished the bus would *never* come.

But it did come, and they began the ride home.

"I forgot to ask you during intermission," she began as they sat hand in hand together, "why that first piece was so familiar."

"Did you ever see the movie *Elvira Madigan*?" Jamie asked.

Kate almost forgot to be surprised by how much Jamie knew. She grinned at him and shook her head. "No, I haven't." The bus turned a corner and pressed her against him. "But *you* have, of course."

"Of course," he agreed with an adorable smile. "Anyway, they used the C-Major Concerto as a theme for the movie. We'll have to see it—you'd like it."

"What's it about?"

"This circus ballerina," he started, then stopped. "I think I'd better not describe it because it might

120

sound too boring, but it really isn't. Trust me."

"I do." *More than you know*, she thought.

Jamie walked Kate to her front door. The only lights on were in her parents' room. This was the moment she had been waiting for—how it felt to kiss Jamie Thompson.

"I'm really glad you came tonight—it made it even better," he said quietly.

"I'm glad I came too," Kate answered.

Jamie took her chin in one hand and looked at her closely. "You're very special."

Kate didn't know what to say. A thousand words were crowding inside her head—all of them about Jamie. She looked up at his smiling, sweet eyes and whispered, "Thank you."

Jamie slowly dropped his hand. "I'll see you tomorrow. Okay?"

Kate blinked once. Wasn't he going to kiss her? She smiled to herself with a sign of resignation. Not Jamie the unpredictable. "Okay. Tomorrow."

She walked into the darkness of her house and upstairs to her room. She felt as if she were in a dream. He hadn't kissed her, but he'd looked at her as if he were kissing her with his eyes. And he had called her *"querida."*

Kate was half tired, but the first thing she did was look up the word in her Spanish dictionary. "Beloved," it said. She lingered on the word. Then she took out some paper to write a quick note to Amy.

Dear Amy:

Actually went out with Jamie tonight. He's even better than I could have hoped for. Went to a Mozart concert. That's right—I did—and loved it. I think I love him too.

Hugs,
Kate

She drifted off to sleep with echoes of silver and gold music interwoven with Jamie's voice.

A couple of days later, Kate promised Jamie that she'd come to soccer practice. He assured her she'd like it.

As she wandered in the labyrinth beneath the bleachers, she remembered the day that she'd seen him here and the way she'd "planted" herself in his way, hoping to "run into" him. Everything was so different now. No more need for dumb games—there probably never was a need for them anyway.

"*Querida*," a familiar voice called to her.

Kate peered into the shadows and saw Jamie. She walked toward him.

He reached out and pulled her gently to him. He held her face softly in his hands. "I've waited a long time for this," he whispered as he bent closer to her.

Kate closed her eyes and felt her dreams come true as she felt Jamie's lips on hers.